Gabrielle Warnock spent her childhood in Cork and Kilkenny, studied at Trinity College Dublin, and lived in England and the U.S., where she first began to write. On returning to Ireland, she settled with her husband and two young sons in County Galway and began submitting her stories to the *Irish Press.* She has had several stories published in Irish newspapers and some have been broadcast on RTE. She was a winner in the Listowel Writer's Week Short Story Competition in 1980 and of a Hennessy Award in 1981. This is her first novel.

FLY IN A WEB

Gabrielle Warnock

poolbeg press

First published 1984 by
Poolbeg Press Ltd.,
Knocksedan House,
Swords, Co. Dublin, Ireland

ISBN 0 905169 63 8

Cover design by Steven Hope
Typeset by Inset Ltd.,
171 Drimnagh Road, Dublin 12.
Printed by Mount Salus Press Ltd.,
Tritonville Road, Dublin 4.

For Keith

Coming home is such a daunting thing.

Lizzie walked slowly by the river. A back-pack hung heavily from her shoulders and seemed to overpower her. The skin around her eyes was swollen, a reaction to the rigours of the night flight from New York. The expression on her face was apathetic. She was already regretting her return, with the callous regret of someone who is making unfavourable early morning comparisons between what she has left behind and what she has arrived to. There was a petrol strike in Dublin. No one had met her at the airport, and at the terminal there had been no taxis. She was walking from the air terminal through the cold, dirty, empty streets of Dublin. The city emanated a discreet, retiring Sunday air. A secretive air. Pharisaism and dissimulation abounded in the reluctantly abandoned bars and dancehalls and the plaintive, calling bells. The tide was out and the exposed guts of the river stank. In an effort to overcome a rising depression, she tried to evoke a nostalgia for the past, but she was too tired. Walking along the quays, she found herself noting things. The green mark of the high tide on the walls and the ladders down to the water. The gulls feeding in the filth. It was as though by noting things she might make herself more aware of her return, but there was no magic in observation. Standing by

O'Connell Bridge in the curiously silenced city with only the bells echoing, she eased the back-pack down from her shoulders and rested it on the pavement against a pillar. Her body, released from weight, seemed to rise lightly, and crossing her arms over her breasts she massaged the two burning patches on her shoulders where the straps of her pack had rubbed. A cheap bag. Her head hummed with tiredness as she leaned on the bridge and her body was chilled through with exhaustion. She had a claustrophobic sense of enclosure on this return.

Sunday

Yesterday I was detached, a citizen of nowhere, America already dismissed, Ireland no more than an emotion of memory. It was Rohan who had been suffused with a last minute tenderness, a sudden desire to prolong contact now that the departure for which he had been waiting impatiently had come. He was overtaken by a wistful series of recollections and his eyes were glossed with commemorative, threatening tears the entire afternoon while we waited in Kennedy Airport for the time to move. He had, nevertheless, come with me all the way from Tucson to New York to make sure I caught the plane and didn't cash in my ticket rather than fly home to Ireland. Such a thorough person. But there he was at Kennedy, with his eyes swimming, while I, on the other hand, was remote, in a curious reversal of our roles. I was more insulated from him than I had been for weeks and I was able to be quite gay and flippant, which must have been aggravating to Rohan. Unseemly. Even on the plane, I was caught up in the excitement of flight.

But on the bridge I was drained. I had arrived and I was totally flat. An object in a view down the river.

I suppose I built up a drama around this return, and I am disappointed. I had to do something once it was decided that I should come home. Rohan made my plans. I could only protect myself by devising some romance out of my destination. Rohan, who majored in psychology and likes to keep up, would have called it further proof of my childish denials of reality. He would have asked me what else I could have expected. He would have told me it was inappropriate of me to expect enthusiasm.

And I was, of course. I expected no less than an excitement to match my own. If not exactly flags, then at least the filling of the tank with contraband petrol from over the Northern Ireland border and a demonstrative surging out to the airport to collect the daughter, the one and only daughter. I was indeed my father's only house-companion for years. But naturally he didn't come. It would have been too demonstrative a thing to do. Quite out of keeping. But that is me again, over-reacting, trying to imagine my father as impulsive as myself and then feeling let down. Who the hell would drive out to the airport in a petrol strike when they know that at least the buses are still mobile? Not someone as cautious as my father. To be honest, most people wouldn't. This is simply further proof of my childish ... But my father is not just cautious. He is also withdrawn. He was always a sad man, almost pitiable. Except that he created a greyness about him and a stifling solitude, which rebuffed the sympathy of those in contact with him. He lost his wife when I was four, and he has always seemed to me to be a man without inner purpose who has concealed his emptiness by appearing a conformer.

But even his conforming goes awry.

This morning, for instance, he went to church, on the

one morning when it might have been more correct for him to remain at home. I have no idea why he goes to church. Rohan would tell me that he goes to church to go to church. Why should you have any idea? Why would he have given you his confidence? The only way to survive living with a person like you is to withhold the parts which one wants to keep intact. You don't recognise your faults *now*, Lizzie. Why would you have recognised them then?

I have always been accustomed to imagine that my father never gave me his confidence because he always viewed me as a child. Sometimes I was afraid that he didn't bother to view me as anything. I think my childhood was wretched. He was such an immensely reserved man that my impetuosity bewildered him. It even slightly disgusted him. My affection seemed animalistic and somewhat obscene to one who wasn't accustomed to the spontaneity of children. Perhaps it was only its direction towards himself that had seemed obscene, but whatever the reason, he was very restrained in his dealings with me. It was not that he was an authoritative man. He never awed me, because I always saw his reserve as weakness, not as power. But he was unapproachable. And I can hear Rohan saying from the bitterness of the last months, "Poor man. His only protection. Being loved by you must have been animalistic enough. Like being constantly licked by a somewhat subservient dog."

When I first told Rohan about my childhood, he was sympathetic. He thought my father must have been an oddball. But latterly he has been vindicating my father and apportioning the blame to me. Rohan became quite cruel. I mean, I can see that my father must have had a fairly unhappy life, without my mother, saddled with a child, housekeepers coming and going. Business worries. But surely it didn't have to be so joyless? And surely my love for him wasn't so unseemly? Rohan says people can only take a certain amount of my sort of love. I become too overwhelming. But that is reference to Rohan and myself. Between my father and myself, it was different. For a start it wasn't ... ah, forget it. Rohan isn't here now. I don't have to justify the fact that I was a child and that I loved the only parent I had and that he did not appear to enjoy the demonstration.

I was waiting in the garden, outside the locked house, when he arrived back from church, stepping up the path in his dark suit, his hair sparser, greyer, his smile as cautious as ever. He hadn't expected me so early, he said. He had to read the lesson. His turn this month. And take up the collection. So even if there had been petrol he could scarcely have met me at the airport because people don't like changing the rota. It was a pity I hadn't arrived sooner, he thought, because then I could have gone to church with him, couldn't I? I would have seen some of my relatives. He seemed vaguely put out that there had been no news of the strike in the States. "I would have thought ... they're always blowing up our strikes in the continental papers. France, you know. Trying to squeeze us out of the EEC."

He looked pleased to see me, but he kissed me only when we had entered the house and the door was closed behind us.

My immediate thought was that I had no business there. I mean, I didn't notice the oddity when I lived with him. When I knew nothing better. But to have gone away, to have had a love affair and then to return, was eye-opening. The house restrains emotions. It defies the rising tones of excitement so that they die, malformed in the throat. I had forgotten the suffocating sensation of entry. And I thought that after two years he might have changed. I've changed so much myself. But he is no different. He offends me with his self-containment and his very distant interest in his daughter. I could see him wondering, as we eyed each other in the hall, how long I would be staying.

It is a dour house. Dark and filled with unmoving, unchanging furniture. The back-pack looked comical, almost garish, propped against the hat stand near the door, and the first movement my father made away from me was to step backwards and trip against the thing. It is an inhuman house. A terrible indictment of my father's existence. Its hopelessness. His negative passage through life. Even the ornaments (the few collected by my mother before her death) have never changed position. The ship-in-the-bottle still lies stranded on the mantelpiece, the pipestand to one side, the ornate silver jug (unused) on the other. The balloon lady sits, a perpetual cripple, on the table between the two sash windows of the sitting room. As a small child I used to lick the coloured china balloons and imagine I could taste a sweetness from them. My father has sat in the same chair each night since I don't know when, and the carpet in front of his chair is rubbed bare from where his shoes rest. He has sat there long enough to collect dust. He smells of the house and the house smells of the dead. The dead flies, crumbling in deserted webs in the high corners of the rooms. The clothes of my dead mother, which still hang in her wardrobe, in the very room where my father sleeps, undisturbed. In my teens I used to think, with brief romanticism, that he slept with her belongings because he was obsessed with my mother. Now I think it is merely rather abnormal. Rohan, when I first told him about the clothes, got excited and talked of necrophilia, but recently he has taken that back. He says perhaps the poor man simply hadn't known how to get rid of all those clothes. The shoes. The bags. The stockings. The pieces of unfinished knitting and sewing. There was a tiny dress, cut out, still pinned (with rusted pins) to its yellowed paper pattern. The dress must have been for me.

Then there were all the dead relatives (for it was a family house) whose portraits hung mustily on walls in passageways, on the stairway, in the diningroom. I am well acquainted with the honesty of those poor innocents who talk in portrait galleries of the eyes following you round the room. It gets to you. It really does. All my childhood was pried upon by those faces with those canny eyes. Watching me down the corridors at night time. Cautioning my movements. Probing my shadows.

Isn't it odd that someone so disinterested should have had such influence? I must have spent most of my childhood studying my father, trying to find ways of pleasing him, of attracting his interest. I am sure I could interpret every nuance of his. After all, I had no one else to watch. Housekeepers came and went so swiftly. They were never there long enough to impinge on me. They didn't care for the atmosphere. It was so lifeless and cold, and there was no female authority to turn to. So it had been only my father and myself. One trying endlessly to be noticed. The other quite unnoticing. Rohan says not unnoticing. Just tired. Certainly too tired ever to be as noticing as I would have required him to be. That may be. Rohan championed my father in our last months. He used him as an invisible ally against me.

I remember how I used to do things that I thought my mother might have done. I would pick flowers for the house. I would even put them on the dressing-table in his room and he would never mention them. Perhaps he thought they were placed there by a housekeeper. I don't know. I was always afraid to ask him.

"I came home to rest."

He didn't ask me why, just nodded his head. He looked tired, but then he always did look tired. I had asked him was he well and he had said yes, fine, but I don't know whether that was a genuine answer or not. It is the answer he always gives to what he presumes to be a rhetorical question.

"I see." As though it was quite normal for someone of my age to retire.

"I was sent home really."

I wanted to tell him about Rohan, but he refused to be drawn. He didn't wish to hear of my difficulties. He wouldn't show the least concern about my state of mind. Not that I think that indicates any lack of love. Equally he wouldn't dream of describing his own state of mind to me. I don't know that he acknowledges states of mind. Certain people don't admit to feelings and he is one of them. I think he finds self-interpretation vulgar. A sign of weakness.

"And now that you're home, what do you plan to do?"

"Jane has asked me to stay."

"Splendid. Not much fun for you here."

We spent an uncomfortable day. We have nothing much to say to one another once we have talked about all the people we know. In his own way he is fond of me, but essentially he distrusts me. He dislikes questioning me about events in my life, because he is afraid I will tell him too much. He wanted to hear impressions of America – its politics, the look of where I lived. The heat. But he wanted to hear nothing personal. He didn't wish to disapprove. If he knew anything of me as a child, he has ceased to know me now. He only knows his memory of me and that is slight enough. And of course, I don't want him to disapprove of me, so I respect his wishes and I tell him nothing.

By evening time we were both feeling affectionate still, but bored. He kept repeating how nice it was to see me again, but he was restless. Uncertain of what he could do in my presence. Afraid to garden for fear I would be hurt. Picking up the paper, reading for five minutes. Dropping it and abruptly starting another conversation.

We went out to a nearby restaurant to eat. I think that during the week he exists on tins of this and that. Those horrible meat pies and soft-boned salmon. But on Sundays he habituates a restaurant in a residential hotel. There is served, even at six o'clock in the evening, a genuine, indigestible Sunday dinner, with damp roast potatoes and an oddly textured, colourless gravy. He brings his own napkin with him, and I saw him furtively cleaning his knife and fork on the linen before starting to eat. The dining room was quite full. Old people and commercial travellers. A place where earlier meals perpetually hover in the air.

As we walked distendedly back through a sombre, little-used park, frequented by the occasional dog and owner, my father said he thought it was time I settled down. In his eyes it is the only thing to do. Settle somewhere, like a fly on dung.

"Are you staying over here for good?" he asked. It was impossible to tell what he thought when I shook my head. I thought perhaps that the urgency vanished from his conversation, but I might be wrong.

"Is Jane expecting you?" he asked as we turned in at the gate. He opened the gate and then stood aside to usher me through before him. A piece of chivalry I had almost forgotten. I nodded.

"Nice for her to have some company." But he didn't sound quite sure. "Odd fellow, Berto. Never could talk to him. Grandiose ambitions, but no aptitude."

I have never heard my father so critical. Jane is my cousin, much older than myself. Her mother was my father's eldest sister. Jane married Berto, whom I can only describe as a slightly dubious person. Shady would be too unkind a word to use. Libellous in fact, because Berto is not a person to do anything illegal on purpose. He would be too frightened, I'm sure. It is just that he gives the impression of attempting to make money in uncomfortable ways, but that may just be the effect of his huge incompetence. He has managed to lose so much money. First of all, he lost his own, and now he has begun to make inroads into Jane's large inheritance. This offends my father. Berto is the sort of person who gives enterprise a bad name. By going about things in the most unacceptable of ways and then failing. He is a person of many aspects, but one feels, in the middle of being enraged by him, an undermining affection.

"What are you going to do, Lizzie?"

I shrugged. I want to be a writer, but I could hardly tell my father that.

"Oh. Something will turn up. I came home to have a holiday. Like being overseas, you know. I need to rest and to water my roots."

"Hmm." He looked bored and sceptical. "You all seem so shiftless these days."

Occasionally I wish I could be the sort of person Dad would like me to be, because I like to please people. He thinks I'm a failure. I was a child of promise. Quite academic, with an actual liking for learning, but I have become a disappointing adult. He was ambitious for me in his enervated way. He thought I might end up teaching teachers, a position which he regards as accolade on accolade. Instead, here I am with no degree, no job and no ambitions. Not even a man behind me. Not that he has ever pressed marriage.

He seems to have taken the attitude to-day that he can do no more for me, and apart from the occasional personal question, he treats me like a visitor, with politeness and reserve.

Monday

Dad took me to the station this morning, having calculated that he could spare the petrol if he missed a meeting this evening. I was touched. He kissed me again, in the echoing, vaulted spaces of the station, while birds flew unconcernedly above us, and he gave a letter to me, his pigeon, to carry to Jane. The post is outrageously expensive and erratic and he was torn between its unreliability and my untrustworthiness. He doesn't like to let people down, and Jane is the sort of person who expects family news. She remembers birthdays, and she sends calendars at Christmas to obscure cousins of Berto's whom she has never met.

"Be sure to give it to her," Dad kept saying to me nervously. His sister used to bully him with good intentions, and Jane reminds him strongly of his sister.

I have never envisaged this return. I thought I had left for good. I felt, when I reached America, that Ireland was a country which one grew beyond. In fact, I spent my last two years at school longing to escape. I felt so constricted. So type-cast. I saw Ireland as a theatre in which the same play was being performed repeatedly with varying degrees of conviction to its captive, helpless audience. And of course, I only had a walk-on part as a double negative. A lapsed, southern Protestant. The play had bored me. So I visited the States for a summer and simply stayed on.

Still, the retreat is only temporary. I feel that I am retiring to the sidelines to bandage up my wounds. It is just that at times America becomes too frenetic to bear. And I have been out of the country long enough to have this cosy, unrealistic view of Ireland as a place of rest. I do not wish them to have the impression that I have come limping home. Whoever they are. Neglected friends in Dublin. Jane. I have returned for certain purposes. I have decided to take myself in hand. Reappraise myself. It is not that I want to settle here. I want to write and how can I get any experiences if I settle? Like Jane. Like Dad. I hate it when they insist that I should be as snared as they are.

I think that so long as I don't feel compelled to stay here, I shan't be restless. So long as they don't use their insidious force. It is when they try to place me in schedules and time limits that I panic and feel I must move on.

The train ride, followed by the bus ride, was too much, and besides, the day outside looked so tempting through the grimy windows that the journey seemed twice as long as it should have been. The bus dropped me off in the village and I left my back-pack in the grocery shop, where, as I remembered, Berto picks up a paper each evening. The shop calls itself a supermarket these days. The man who took the pack from me remembered my face, which made me feel badly, since I had no recollection of his. He couldn't remember my name though, or who was my connection down here, so when I asked if I could leave the pack with him for my cousin to collect, he had to ask me who my cousin might be, which I felt was one up for me. And then, when he had me placed, he came out from behind the counter and shook my hand and said he'd heard I had been staying in the States, and wasn't it well to be back and he hoped I would be staying. Then he gave me one of those great, whipped icecreams to eat on my walk to Jane's house. I felt like a child again, and it was very silly, but I had tears in my eyes when I walked out of the village, past the petrol station with its closed sign hanging half off its hinge.

That walk to Jane and Berto's house is beautiful. I used to come here often as a child. I had forgotten the beauty. Or maybe I never noticed. The weather helped of course. The day was really most beguiling. A light breeze frothed and shook the whitethorn blossom and rippled the grasses in the ditch. The scent of the blown hawthorn flowers caught densely in the nostrils. It was a painter's day. Rivers of colour meandered and trickled through broken clouds, and, inevitably, somewhere a lark sang. There was rising heat shimmering on the road, though it is only May. It was a sharply evocative walk, recalling childhood holidays, and I did childish things. I bit the bottom out of my cone and sucked the icecream down from the top through the narrowing tube of biscuit. I stripped the flowering heads from the stalks of early grass which I pulled as I walked, and I blew dandelion clocks. I was mesmerised into relaxation and I remember whistling. Bits from a piano concerto, I can't for the life of me recall which one. Probably I didn't know its name. Rohan used to play the piano in our apartment and I used to annoy him intensely by inadvertently humming with the tune. I am one of those people who picks up tunes easily, but in an unobservant way. I do not recognise the different composers and I always remain silent when good music is discussed in that pompous way which people of certain knowledge can convey to those of uncertain knowledge. Rohan says I am an ignorant sensualist. The lark had dropped down and was no longer singing, so my whistling competed with nothing.

It was so peaceful to stroll along a country road with hot, scented air pressing in on me and warmth on my head. I can't remember when I last walked on a road so crowded on either side with vegetation. And the warmth itself was just right. Tucson had been growing oppressively hot.

There were discrepancies though. A very ugly grotto in the shape of a concave heart has been erected on Geraghty's corner. Further along the road, the Cistercian Abbey has been wounded with messages. H BLOCK, in lettering a foot high, and above that, a smaller, fainter message advising BRITS OUT. It reminded me of those reactions in the States. They couldn't understand my disinterest (as they saw it). What's going on in your country? Asked above the faint reverberations of Vietnam and falling presidents. My explanation of distance from events came back so smugly. It is so difficult to explain, I would say, and out would struggle the platitudes. The troubles don't impinge on us down south. No, really they don't. You wouldn't believe how different the two sides of the Border are. These scribblings? Community murals. Graffiti. No more. I used to panic when people questioned me. Where do you stand? I didn't know. I still don't. As a southern Protestant, the more informed would press, and I would shrug. But they rarely got so far as to find out my religion. I preferred to let them assume what they would. Later, Rohan taught me to put an armour of deflection on myself and I would parry their questions with questions of my own. Rohan taught me a lot. He was quite a mental subversive in those early days.

I walked quickly past the Gate Lodge at the bottom of their drive. They are turning it into a shop. It still looks just the same from the outside, but there were two vans and a lorry parked beyond the wall, and I could hear the sounds of people working inside.

You know how it is that certain houses invade your bones. For all the last six months in the States, I saw the Lodge as my refuge. At the time, I needed the thought of that house. I needed a retreat. It wouldn't have been possible. Jane would have been so hurt had I asked to live in the Lodge instead of staying up at the house with them. And Berto would have droned on about insurance and rates and drains until all the spontaneity would have vanished from the idea.

I love their house too. The big house that is. The one they live in. Despite them, it has character. It was a rectory. A solid, Georgian rectory, with a destructively damp basement. It came on the market because this parish was amalgamated with three others and Dobbs, the man here, retired. The church authorities, the bishop, I suppose, waited for his retirement before closing down his church, but Dobbs must have resented their patience. He knew himself to be superfluous. Dobbs had not been a gardening man. He had planted some hazel by the house when he first came, presumably as a wind-break, and then he had left the ensuing scrub to encroach as it would around the house. The people in the village said he had been a very solitary man. He rarely fraternised, even with his few Protestant neighbours, and led what sounded like an oddly idle and reclusive life. He must have seen such a futility to his life's work as a clergyman in the dwindling numbers of his parishioners. He had come as a young man and had probably not expected to remain here. But he was left to decline with his parish. The house had mirrored his decay. He had gone to Dublin to live with a daughter after his retirement and had soon died.

I know what Dad means about grandiose ambitions. Last time I was staying here, Berto and Jane were just recovering from an abortive mushroom scheme. Mushrooms in the basement. Berto was going to make his fortune. He spent a fortune starting off. Berto has never denied any of his projects the money necessary to float them. Rows and rows of fish boxes stacked one on top of the other, right up to the ceiling, in what had been one of the wine cellars. He must have had about two hundred boxes. He was, he said, starting small. Testing the market. Later, he planned to expand until the entire basement had become a mushroom factory. He planned to export them. And the trouble is, he was so convincing. I mean, he had really done quite a lot of research into the subject of growing mushrooms. He knew all the pitfalls. And he fell into most of them. How, if the boxes weren't properly sealed, they would rot. And despite his efforts, those boxes rotted. Probably the effects of their vitriolic manure. He and Jane had to make this truly vast compost heap in the courtyard outside the basement door. Soaked straw bales and dearly bought horse manure. Berto had been all for buying yearlings, breaking them in and selling them as three year olds, or four year olds, I can't remember the details, thereby dovetailing two enterprises. Luckily, Jane persuaded him to wait on that one. Anyway, they spent days just filling the fish boxes. Carrying two hundred boxes filled with heavy, damp compost down the narrow broken steps to the basement. And of course there was no electricity down there. Candles and torches.

Berto was cutting costs by not bringing electricity down to mushrooms since his book said they could survive in the dark. They planted the spores, or whatever it is you do with spores, and the mushrooms germinated by the thousand and then developed the most disfiguring moulds and worm holes. The compost hadn't heated up enough and all the bacteria were alive and multiplying. They couldn't even sell the mushrooms in the village, not to mind exporting them to Saudi Arabia or whatever part of the world it was Berto had in mind. And there were only so many desiccated mushroom stews, mushrooms on toast, mushroom patés that they could consume themselves. Then, since they weren't picking them as they matured, the mushrooms began to rot, and the stench in the basement was like that of trapped, dead rats. The smell percolated right up to the third floor of the house. So they had to take all their boxes and empty them around the garden. Now Jane says she is incessantly picking mushrooms in the rose beds where really they look most attractive, if rather coy.

Dad always feels sorry for Jane, but I think she is just as bad as Berto. At least, she is bad *for* Berto. She encourages him. She leads him to believe that all his ideas are swans. But then, as I said, he can be so believable. Perhaps she just believes him and is constantly surprised by disappointment. You would think that with all these schemes they would be quite exciting, unusual people, but in fact they are very conforming and they take themselves most seriously.

The amount of money they must have spent on the house and the garden. They have obliterated what few memories remained of the old man, and the house has certainly revived wonderfully, returning to its original elegance. Indeed, I imagine it probably surpasses it.

The tall, cool rooms, the eight-paned windows. Light floods the house, and I think that is probably what struck me most as a child, coming from my own gloomy, overlooked house in Dublin. And then the curved banisters with their secreted carvings which fitted into the curve of my hand. Walking up the shallow, weathered steps to the front door made me lurch with the recollected wonder I had for the house.

They bulldozed the hazel scrub when I was quite young. One of the first years I came here, I used to play solitary games of Robin Hood in the thickets, and the next year my forest had gone. Friar Tuck and Maid Marion and Robin Hood had been eradicated like pests. Then they had called in a professional landscaper to give them the right garden for the house. Not a single idea of their own in the whole of the two acres. Once, when the garden was growing towards its brief prime, it was photographed for a magazine, and Jane posed with a basketful of flowers (arranged by the photographer) at a patio table in the courtyard. She still has copies of the magazine, with its discoloured pages. Now the garden is growing beyond control. Berto attacks it with bursts of enthusiasm, and then he succumbs to despair, and when Berto is in despair about something he becomes paralysed and is unable to cope with the object of his despair. So the hazel begins to creep insidiously back through the shrubs and roses are being strangled by convolvulus.

Jane said she was thrilled to see me. She talks in superlatives. She always looks so clean and bright. She is in her forties, but she has one of those ageless, unformed faces. The sort of face which never knew a spot. It has lines of surprise, freckles and streaks of laughter, but nothing has cut deeper than that. She is one of those people who changes from the skin out when visitors are expected, and when I arrived, slightly sticky from my walk, over-tired from yesterday's plane journey, she overwhelmed me with impeccable kindness.

I am very fond of Jane, but she has no subtlety. If one wants to make a point, one has to be as overwhelming as herself. Having discovered that Berto was at a meeting, I said that I simply had to have a bath and lie down, because I was absolutely exhausted and I didn't want to look the most frightful wreck when Berto arrived home.

To be safe, I dozed on my bed until I heard the sound of Berto's car returning. I didn't even imagine that he might be stuck for petrol. People like Berto always have sources. There is always this fellow or that fellow who owes him a favour. He managed to make the gravel spray out from under the wheels of his car with a most luxurious sound when he stopped the car near the front door. It must take some practice and stage management.

I waited until I imagined that he was sitting with a drink before I descended to the drawing room.

Even with me, about whom he has mixed feelings, Berto cannot refrain from acting gallantly. I believe he is unsure of me because he senses that I don't take him absolutely seriously. It makes me a threat. Jane says I am wrong in thinking that Berto dislikes me. She says he is very fond of me. Jane is naive. He isn't as petty as that, in fact. He could live with the thought that I don't take him seriously, but he is afraid that I will infect Jane with my scepticism. Also, he so adores Jane that he resents intruders and I have been intruding for years. I really think he would have resented his own children. They have none. I used to think they couldn't have any, but lately I have wondered. Anyway, as I say, he had to act gallantly. He took my face in his hands and kissed me on both cheeks and told me I looked quite stunning. Which is palpably untrue. I have never in my life looked stunning. His double embrace, his actual name, are affectations. His maternal grandmother, I think, was Italian, and Berto has acquired some mannerisms.

He was looking like a swindler this evening. He always looks disreputable when he puts on a suit. Fresh from a meeting on tourism, he was talking volubly, as the economic spokesman for Ireland. One of the few successful enterprises he is involved with is a company which rents holiday houses. Very thatched. Very ethnic. Very pricey. Foreigners throng to them. But this year tourism is slumping and the foreigners are booking only patchily. Jane says early days yet, it's only May, but Berto looks gloomy and pulls a face. He has been sobered by his fellow directors. This year looks bad. "Not a year for opening a shop," he said, looking significantly at Jane, and she, sitting on a chair with her legs crossed, waved a hand at him.

"Oh nonsense, Berto. Don't be such a death's head. There'll never be a right time if we listen to all the pundits. My glass is empty. Be a darling, would you?"

I sat with a gin and tonic, my eyes half-closed, while Berto, remembering his manners, talked to me about an America I don't know, that he knows I don't know, but it's the only one he can imagine so he talks about it anyway. The rich eastern belt of business. He talked of the poverty in this country, and its greed, its dissipation, and all the while he was smoking a cigar straight from the Third World and he was jabbing it at Jane and myself to punctuate his remarks.

"We could learn a lesson or two from America, couldn't we, Lizzie?"

"I don't know, Berto. I was a drop out."

I am not prepared to stay here long. Which would doubtless please poor Berto if he knew. I had forgotten how dauntingly righteous the pair of them can be. It must be more than a factor of age. Despite their endless experiments and ventures, they seem to have remained mentally static for so many years. Their personalities and their attitudes are rigid and confined. And they are cloyingly contented. I cannot trust such contented people. I suspect that one can only be so contented if one never subjects oneself to close interrogation. Their contentment must come from seeing themselves in too good a light. They are invariably correct in their attitudes. The yardstick by which other people must be measured. I thought I would be immune to them by now, but I find I am lying in bed, seething. I had forgotten how much they could annoy me.

They have given me an attic room, which is one of the most undisturbed rooms of the house. It is also one of the hottest. Tonight it is stifling, although the window has been open since this afternoon. All the moths in the garden have been attracted by the open window and the light within, and despite the drawn curtains they have seeped into the room and are swirling insanely around the Victorian lampshade of frilly glass.

This much has changed at least. Before, Berto and Jane used to suck me into their plans. Now, at least, I am strong enough to remain alienated. I may not argue. I may remain silent, but I dislike their ideas. I despise them.

I used to think that Jane was more like me. I used to think of her as a reluctant chameleon. That she suited her behaviour to her environment. That she had adopted Berto's beliefs as a sort of self-protection, and within a certain framework I couldn't blame her. I mean, if one wanted to survive an existence with Berto, one would have to succumb to his way. I used to think that she had been drawn against her judgement into acceptance of his attitudes. That her first line of defence had been silence, and the silence had turned to apathy and the apathy had become acquiescence. Now I am not at all sure that she hasn't been abetting him all through.

They want me to be the manager of their craft shop in the Lodge. I said, no, no, no.

And Jane looked reproachfully at Berto, who had brought the subject up, and said that really, he should have more consideration. Couldn't he see that I was far too tired to talk about business tonight? We would discuss it when we were all fresher. I said there was nothing to discuss. I most certainly wasn't too tired to say no, and I had said no. Jane said that well, we would see, and then, to change the subject, she asked me how my father was. Had he sent a letter? They were much more interested in my father than they were about my two years in the States.

"Really, how is your father? Poor Richard. We must have him to stay. He misses out on family life so much. I never could see why he didn't marry again. Lucy died so young."

That caused me suppressed amusement, because yesterday afternoon, when we were talking of Jane and Berto, my father had sighed and had said that really, he should make the effort and visit poor Jane and Berto. They were always asking and he was always putting off the day.

"He's awfully busy at the moment," I said.

"Oh, for heaven's sake."

But I think Jane was relieved at my excuse. Family life? My father detests family life.

The implication from Jane that, given a good mood, I could be persuaded to manage their horrible shop – this is what has made me seethe. And to think that they were treating me cautiously this evening. They bully people. They are so certain their own ideas are right that they have no compunction about attempting to force them on others. They think that the responsibility would do me good.

I have come home particularly to be myself. I do not want to be manipulated by anyone. I want, for once, to be allowed to explore my own potential without interference. I am too malleable. Too anxious to please other people. I am only just finding out that pleasing other people doesn't even have the expected results. In the States, Rohan could wind me around his little finger. Every time he changed, I would change along with him, and he still got tired of me.

Despite my weariness, I have ended up sitting by the open window, with the light off, resting in the breeze. The birds are thrown by the brightness of the night, and there is an occasional tentative song of surprise.

Thursday

To me, this household seems obsolete. I have been here for some days now. I know the pattern and it seems a life of such sterility. They seem to see themselves as real, and things beyond as somehow comic and unconnected with themselves. It is as though nothing matters beyond the perimeters of their own existence. Everything is subjected to some imagined form and tradition.

I think that Jane has created this life-style deliberately. Almost as an art-form. She doesn't wish to be disturbed. And yet, things force themselves upon her and make her restless. She would not admit that she gets frightened, bored or confused.

I suspect that Berto loses money. (Not his fault of course, poor darling. No one is making any money these days. Bogmen running the economy. We're all losers.) I think that Berto keeps her ill-informed. It is not that she tells me these things. She does not confide. But over the years, from half-spoken conversations between herself and Berto when they have either forgotten or discounted my presence, I have surmised these things. I think that Jane feels helpless and is trying to imprint herself safely within her house. She pretends confidence in Berto and she is lonely.

She and I were in the drawing room, sitting on a refurbished chaise-longue, drinking coffee.

"I've always thought that to own a shop would be the greatest fun. I love people. I love talking to people. And we see so few here. We're so far from everything. Sometimes I wish we were closer to ... and then I think to myself, well, closer to what? I mean, what is there really to which one needs to be close? When one analyses one's desires. And the house. It would be quite impossible to leave the house. But occasionally, it's so ... remote. And you see, a shop ...?" Her hands were stretching and twisting as she talked. Jane has grown thinner in the last two years. Her engagement ring often swivels around on her finger so that the stone hangs into the palm of her hand. And she has developed the habit of swirling it in circles round her finger with her thumb.

"A shop," she continued, "would be so perfect. I mean, I can't think why we haven't thought of a shop before now. But I suppose, with Berto's mother living in the Lodge, it simply never occurred to us. I do believe I have a head for business, Lizzie, and it would be so nice, wouldn't it, to have a steady source of profit?"

Somehow, I almost tended to believe her when she said she had business instincts. Despite her lack of confidence, she has organizational flair. She likes to be in command.

I was sitting beside Jane, making reticent noises. I was so afraid of sounding enthusiastic and being drawn into the business of shop-keeping myself. The drawing room is a lovely room, curved at one end. It adjoins the dining room, to which it is connected by folding doors. The dining room, at the opposite end, is also curved so that the two rooms make a stretched oval. Jane likes to keep the folded door ajar, even when only two people are in the drawing room, because the glimpse of that other room retreating to its curve extends the possibilities of perspective so much. It makes for a draught about the legs, but she doesn't seem to notice the discomfort.

"More coffee?" she asked and I nodded.

"Please."

She lives her life with style. We not only have ground coffee, but it is made in a silver pot (from whose contents one can occasionally detect the taste of silver polish). Unwhipped cream in a matching silver jug and thick, brown crystals of sugar in a silver bowl. Tiny, silver lions lie at the base of each of the handles on the three utensils, while the domed lid of the coffee pot has a larger lion as the handle. The whole pot overheats and burns the hand. Made before they discovered the idea of insulating the handles with wooden stoppers.

A woman – Mrs. Cleary, from the village – comes to clean each day. To help maintain the dream. Yesterday, Jane said in reply to some question of mine, that it was the house itself which called for a certain standard of living. She said that it demanded a grace and a service which is now out of fashion. As though the house had a soul. I laughed when she said that and remarked that I thought she was living in cloud-cuckoo-land. I also thought, though I didn't say it, that she is a superlative snob, and she has convinced herself, because it suits her aspirations, that the inanimate house is the dictator, whereas she, in reality, is the source of grandeur. Her life looks utterly pointless to me and I suspect that she begins to find it lacking herself. She is, after all, intelligent. She can't deceive herself completely. She knows her origins. A large semi in Templeogue. The elegance of the house started as an amusement. Quite exciting. Different. But it palls now. I think all these things, but I say very little. One of Jane's habits which annoys me is that though I am reticent about her way of life, she is critical of mine.

Because she has recently discovered an interest, the damned craft shop, she now feels that her whole life has been leading methodically to this. She thinks that at twenty-one I should know where I am going. By now I should have put aside childish whims. I should have managed to adjust to the unpleasant aspects of society. Why, at twenty-one she married Berto. (And if that is not adjusting to the unpleasant aspects of society, I don't know what is. That is positively lying down and rolling in the unpleasant aspects. I don't mean to be unkind to Berto, but the thought of condemning oneself to a lifetime of Berto at my age. I'm sure Jane did not mean me to take the implications I did from her remark.) She says it is a good thing to adjust a little this way and that way, to fit into the recognised pattern of things.

She was serious.

Why is it that other people have ambitions and a sense of order, while I flounder in a bog of uncertainties? That I suffer from drift and indecision seems to disturb Jane. She says I make her feel uncomfortable. Perhaps she is jealous. Perhaps she sees me freer than herself and would like to see me captured so that she wouldn't have to envy me any more.

Her self-confidence has been ruffled recently and my arrival serves to agitate her further. She thinks that I have changed.

"You used to be amenable."

As I say, I am a malleable person, but I have really decided to harden and Jane is most frustrated by the fact that I am still refusing to act as the manager for her shop. She is honestly baffled by my reluctance. She discounts my real reasons as impossible, so she can only imagine that I have other, hidden reasons for not taking up the offer. She cannot believe that I honestly wish to drift for the entire, long summer.

"But you have already been drifting for two years, Lizzie."

To call a love affair drifting. But Jane likes solid results, and there are no results that she can see from this affair. I can't explain my reasons to her. She is like my father. She shies away from discussion of personal feeling. I can't very well say to her things like wanting to discover my soul, or wishing to work out my own philosophy without interference. She would be embarrassed. I would feel awkward myself. So I have to mutter unsatisfactorily about drifting, and she in turn is hurt, because she thinks that really I don't want to be connected with one of their enterprises, or perhaps that I no longer care for them. Before, she has always assumed that she is liked by other people, but her assumption has been undermined. Not initially by me. By a potential supplier. She has gone quite far in researching her enterprise. She has told me of all the trade fairs and craft exhibitions she attended during the winter. She even attended a short course on small business techniques. Despite myself, I have been fascinated by all that she has done. So un-Jane like. Which makes it all the more unbelievable to her that I should not be keen to join her. We'd be equal partners, she keeps saying to me. When Jane is enthusiastic about something, she cannot believe the apathy of others. She becomes wounded if they are less than wholehearted.

Anyhow. This potential supplier. He is apparently a potter. Lives alone in a cottage on the far side of the village, above the harbour. He moved into this derelict place about three years ago and renovated the cottage with his own hands. Since then, he has lived there like a recluse. He is very anti-social. Doesn't mix at all. Somehow, Jane heard that he was a potter, and being on the lookout for local crafts she went along to see him. Her visit made her uneasy. For a start, she couldn't place him. She doesn't have a compartment which fits him (she has so few compartments) and an unplaced person disturbs her. She would like to be able to write him off as a layabout, as this would leave her free to disapprove of him and then she could forget about him. But she can't do that. His pottery was beautiful. She says it is far above the usual standard. Things lived in the hand. Jane held a cat in her hand, and it vibrated with pleasure. She could have sworn it did. Also, his accent is cultured, and given Jane's inclination towards snobbery she can hardly dismiss such an obvious product. She is in a dilemma about him, the more so because he seems to despise her. He is not even anxious to sell any of his work. He becomes attached to his own creations. She has been to see him twice, and each time he seems to be waiting for her to leave. He tells her nothing about himself and he asks no questions of her. I think this piques her, as his reserve makes her appear as crudely inquisitive. "He can't be shy. He must be boorish. I have to make conversation for two, Lizzie."

He makes her nervous.

He is constantly scraping at pieces of wood with a knife. Whittling. He is, she says, one of those people who cannot stand alone. He always has to be propped against something. A wall, a bench, a doorway. It makes him somehow more sinister. I think that what gets her most is the fact that she is prepared to like him and he is not prepared to like her. She is interested in him and would like to find out more about him. She genuinely admires his work. She would like to purchase some of his pottery. Whereas, he doesn't give a damn about her. She was talking about this quite indignantly while we were finishing coffee, and I did feel sorry for her. I said I knew the type. He feels he knows all he needs to know about her already. He has opted out of his particular social bracket, and once out, he has immediately lumped those that remain under the same heading and attributes to all of them the same faults, the same dullness, the same unworthiness. He is suspicious of them all. He sounds most irritatingly supercilious. I must say though, I would like to meet him myself. After all, I imagine I must be closer to his choice of existence than to the existence of Jane and Berto.

I think Jane recognises this, which is why she is so uncertain. She isn't sure of my allegiance any more and it is making her slightly aggressive towards me. She tries to force my opinions out of me, while I try to keep my own counsel, so as not to offend her. If it wasn't for the fact that she has been pressing me to come and spend the summer with them, I think she would be inclined to accuse me of sponging on her. She is funny. Because she also feels guiltily that I will think she only asked me to come on account of the shop. And even if that was true, she would hate me to think so, because it is not the sort of thing which relatives should do to each other.

But to return to the potter. She finds him odd, and it frets her. He doesn't display what she considers to be normal, social behaviour and this frightens her. One of the things which upsets her more than anything is the fact that when she smiles at him, he doesn't smile back. I know what she means. It is most disconcerting. A rebuff of your advance, of your possible friendship. Just recounting to me how she had smiled at him, and how he had looked impassively back at her, made her angry, and she then went on to remark that he was really rather disgusting. He smells of sweat and his teeth are dirty. He should know better. As I say, she is unsettled by him. She wants to know his background. She doesn't even know which persuasion he is, as she puts it. I said to her that he was probably agnostic like myself, but she withered me with a look. I knew exactly what she meant. I was merely being obtuse. Was the background ours? She didn't want to have to say it, because she finds the religious divisions too delicate a subject to talk about. Another area of guilt in fact. Jane doesn't like to admit that she feels more comfortable in the presence of other Protestants, because she thinks private, confused, uncharitable thoughts about Catholics. She doesn't really know any. She is afraid of being caught out. She is a social Protestant. She goes to church every third Sunday or so, and that suffices her. I doubt that she has ever really contemplated her religion. I also doubt that she could list the main differences between the Protestant and the Catholic Articles of Faith. Neither could I.

At least, she says, will I come with her the next time she visits this man. Because she must have some of his pottery. She must. I agree with alacrity. I am curious to meet the person who can so unsettle Jane.

The atmosphere in this house is claustrophobic. I cannot contemplate writing here. I am seriously thinking of cutting short my visit, though I can't imagine where I should go from here. I can't, in all politeness, leave in less than a fortnight.

Tuesday

After last night, I had to escape the house for the day. Luckily the weather co-operated. I was eating my breakfast, late, and Jane was saying, while she cleared around me, that she hoped I would bear in mind what she and Berto had been saying last night, and that she hoped I didn't think they had been interfering. Well, she knew I hadn't liked the conversation from the sullenness of my face, but ... They had only been trying to help, and being that much older they felt they had certain experience which I still lacked, and that while I might not see their point of view immediately, over time I might agree.

I could tell that she might continue thus all day, justifying herself and trying to wear me down, so I simply said that of course I didn't mind being given advice and I thought they were more than kind. Then I said I would love to take some sandwiches and go off for a hike. This diverted her, and she immediately fetched from a cupboard a little tin of paté for me to use in my sandwiches. She is really very kind, and I feel badly that I am abusing her kindness by not falling in with her plans and by being inwardly critical.

Sky, hills, sea, hills, sky. A circling, turning, giddy view. Seagulls and jackdaws sketched loops across the sky and two-dimensional boats clung to the surface of the sea. The thin, tumbled walls of rotund stones were speckled with sun-coloured lichens and occasional thorn trees crouched in their fragile shelter.

I chose the beach. There is something sumptuous about a deserted beach. One's unaccompanied footsteps in the sea-washed sand. In the sheltered curve of the lagoon, I lay against a ledge of scaly-capped rocks, using my rolled up jersey as a pillow for my head.

At that angle, with the sun shining on my half-shut lids, I felt I was spinning in a wheel. I had taken off my shoes and socks, and as I lay there my toes worked back and forth assiduously in the sand, hollowing out channels through the damp, sticky grains.

I miss Rohan.

Jane and Berto's kindness is impossible. I cannot cope with their overbearing concern for me. You see, Jane has always felt responsible for me. My mother, as I have said, died when I was scarcely more than an infant, and I have always been free to make my home with Jane. Mostly I have come here for summer holidays. She believes that she should have had more influence over my decision to stay in the States for two years. She thinks that my stay there was a mistake, and that perhaps she should have flown out to persuade me to come home. I can imagine Rohan's face.

I can't make her understand that I was simply exploring. I spent a year in college, and was frantic to see the States, so I went over to New York in the summer, to one of those temporary student jobs. Then I bought a Greyhound ticket and set off. I met Rohan down the Grand Canyon, went to stay with him in Tucson, and never moved on. Jane says the less said about it the better. If people ask. I don't want to give myself a bad name. Really. She said all those things and I thought she was joking and burst out laughing, and then she was quite offended. She said I never did take her seriously and that maybe America was different, but round here, people were still highly principled.

Oh dear.

I can't bring myself to say how much I despise the way Jane and Berto live. I feel it would be too ungrateful. Besides, I have always thought that people are unnecessarily destructive in their relationships with others. They are far too quick to criticise. But if I can accept that Jane lives in what, to me, is an unpalatable way, why then can *she* not accept *my* way? At one point last night she leaned forward to put her hand on my arm and said of course she knew I only lived the way I did in the States because I had no choice, and she herself didn't hold it against me at all. I was nonplussed. Totally silenced. I simply had nothing to say. That she could take my love affair in her hand and crumple it. And since I was silent, she took this for acquiescence, and she went on to say that I shouldn't have been afraid to come home. They would not have shunned me. So apparently it was thought that I was too ashamed to come home. And of course, instead of saying that I loved Rohan, which would have been the positive thing to say, I only said that I had not wanted to come home, which could have been interpreted in a number of ways. Under the circumstances, I simply didn't wish to mention Rohan's name. It would have sounded too ridiculous. But I wish Rohan could have heard Jane. He has always thought that I exaggerated my family.

Jane and Berto think that I should live with them for a year or so, help to run the shop, and re-establish myself in Ireland, where I do, after all, have a large circle of acquaintances and relatives. They both state most insistently that I must do something. That I can't continue to drift. That advice from Berto, who has not just drifted but has lurched from disaster to disaster ever since I have known him. I don't think either of them realises in the slightest how funny the advice sounds, coming from them. They think that so long as you are doing something, you're safe. They adore one another, and they are very bad for one another. They make incessant excuses for each other, so that if one falters momentarily and has the grace to suffer any self-doubts, the other immediately pushes them on and dissipates the doubts. So they never have long enough to make any self-discoveries. I would go so far as to say that they distrust thought processes which involve an input of time and no practical output.

It is odd, but they try to treat my affair with Rohan as though I am ashamed of it. Jane tries to pretend that it never occurred. She seems to convince herself that I am still a virgin, and she was speaking of my being able to meet lots of nice young men, as though I am to be unleashed into local society under the guise of innocence. Berto, on the other hand, takes the pragmatic view that a finished affair is dead and might as well never have occurred. He did say, in his cautious way, that I might be advised to live more carefully over here, as this is still such a closed, vindictive society. Repeating Jane, he said that one didn't want to be labelled in any way. It is better to be circumspect, he said. And when I asked him if he meant hypocritical, he nodded and put his finger to his lip.

Jane says it would be good for me to have a job. You can't just vegetate, Lizard, she says. You mustn't become a hibernating Lizard. Lizard is a childhood name she uses for me. As a child I was evasively agile. I still am. I also have the lizard's habit of lying very still in the sun. She pointed out the pertinent fact that I could do with the money. I just let her talk, since it pleases her to make plans. But I do feel that they are invading. Is it so selfish to wish to spend a summer alone? Thinking. They begin to make me feel enmeshed. They are being awfully sensible, and it is difficult for me to disagree with them without sounding childish and petulant.

The sand on the beach is a grey sand. It does not light up as it should in the sun. It is a heavy sand, as the particles are large, and the area most recently left bare by the receding tide looks caught in static ripples. In the depressions between the ripples, trapped water sinks below the sand with barely audible bubbling sounds. I had intended to walk, but in the end I lay still, absorbing the noise. The pound and suck of the sea.

In Tucson, Rohan and I twice planned to cross California, to see the Pacific. But we never did go. At first there was never enough money. Later, when he offered to take me, I knew it was a last offer, a panacea, and I refused to go. I would like to have seen the Pacific.

I ate my sandwiches and threw crusts to the gulls. They ignored the crusts, which were instead soaked up by the crabbed, creeping, tip-toe wavelets which trickled faintly down the sand. While the birds swept negligently overhead.

On my way back I climbed over the foot-rasping rock to where the pier juts, bent-legged, out into the harbour, and I sat on a rusting bollard to watch a boat coming in. The fisherman had two lobsters under the boards and he offered me one, but I couldn't bear the thought of carrying home a live lobster and hearing its pincers clicking and scraping on other parts of its shell. Besides, I hadn't enough money.

The man wasn't local, but when I asked him where he

lived, he jerked his thumb towards the hill above the harbour.

"You're not originally from here," I said and he smiled, bending to catch the lobsters by their humped backs.

"No matter," he said, "I don't take up much space."

The potter, I presumed, as I walked away from the pier. He seemed nicer than Jane's description. He did, after all, smile.

There were two old men, sitting on a blue-painted, blistered Council bench in the memory-taunting, inflexible heat of the sun. They hummed words as I approached and I smiled at them as I continued by. Oh God, how despicable to be old. That old, when all you can do is remember.

The day was throbbing hot. I passed up the village street, and various dogs, exhausted with heat, lay by doorways, with vivid, lolling tongues and tails waving swag-swag, fanning the endless, tormenting flies.

The village is by the sea, but it looks almost as though the sea saw the village from a distance and has crept in to shelter close by the houses. For the tide enters this bay by way of a narrow neck cut through a low reef of rocks, so that the bay forms an oval lagoon of calm water. Beyond the lagoon, the sea spurts and sucks against the reef, even on the gentlest of days, and the neck makes a treacherous entry for fishing boats. But once inside they are safe. The wind flicks no more than white foals in here and the sea rides slack against the harbour wall.

It is a poignant village. Everybody's fancied childhood. There is a terrace of tall, thin, coloured houses down on the quay. At the harvest and the hunter moons and during winter storms, the basements flood and the rats swim. A mill decays nearby, its tidal race choked with seaweed and old metal. Blue Council benches defying comfort. The ancient pension men. Herds of children. Herds of dogs. Men on the dole. Women who lean, arms folded, at the entrances to their houses, watching the children, watching nothing, watching each other.

Difficult to step out of line here. And on a rainy day water runs in the gutters from the top of the village to the bottom of the village. And the people at the bottom of the village shop downtown. And the people at the top of the village shop uptown. They say that the top of the village is healthier. Less damp. Windier. The germs are scattered. The harbour rats are said to be dirtier than the field rats. Descended from the plague rats which came here in ships.

They call the place a town, not a village. It is a universal town. People come here touring and they are disappointed. They find it too like home and they move on. There is a local saint, a cure for warts, a gombeen man and Berto says there is a whore. I don't know.

I stopped for an icecream in the supermarket and Mick, the grocer, came and stood outside on the pavement with me while I ate it. Mick is the only friend I've made since I came home. I see him every day because I come down to collect the paper on Jane's bicycle. I like the fact that his mind is not enclosed. This town makes him impatient. Talk about feuding. They tried to set up a co-op in the place once, and it fell apart after six months. There are people not talking over it yet. Mick is quite proud of the fact. He said it shows that the place isn't bloody Russia. You can't push this lot around. Individuals, the lot of them. They'll not set up one of their bloody state communes here. Mick is all for the autonomy of the individual. Better for his business. Thing is, he says, that there are a lot of bastards in the town who wouldn't half mind setting up a nice, rigid society, with all the lads kow-towing and singing in unison. But each of them wants to be the one at the top. The one directing operations. So they are self-regulating in a way. No one gets away with a trick.

It is easier to combine in condemnation. I was asking Mick about the fisherman down on the pier, and he rubbed his hand over his face, catching his nose up in the web of skin between two stretched fingers.

"Not liked," he said, his mouth still beneath the palm of his hand, and he looked down at me and winked.

"Works too hard. Catches too many lobsters. While they're all still asleep."

His asceticism offends people. He lives, by choice, on the edge of poverty, and this is discomfiting to his neighbours. Around here, where people are acquiring the first luxuries of affluence ever, he is regarded with uncomfortable contempt. There is great emphasis on maximising your talents, and that he has, according to gossip, abandoned a good job to live such a life, is regarded with derision.

"He doesn't go to Mass. People distrust him. There are great rumours of course. They say he is recovering from a nervous breakdown, but nobody knows for certain."

The Lodge was deserted on my return. There is a low stone wall between the Lodge and the main drive, and I sat there, on a cushion of creeping stone crop dwarfed by the first of a line of towering, heady beeches which ascend the drive to the rectory. I was pretending that the Lodge was mine. The garden was darkened, not only by the trees, but also by the solid evening shadow of the lodge itself, and the lawn, which is stippled with daisies and woven with ladies' bedstraw, looked cool to lie on after the stirred dust of the road.

I have been carrying a notebook around with me for days, in the hope that I would be inspired to write something. I had really meant to write down on the beach today, but instead I lay there like a stranded whale, mooning about Rohan. While I was sitting on the wall I wrote a couple of lines, describing the beach, but the biro began to leak. The heat of carrying it around in my back pocket made the ink expand and it refused to write and then, when I looked down, my hands were covered in ink.

How does one set about writing? I don't even have a subject. Or an object. Perhaps I should study Jane and Berto. Hang onto their every word and movement. Write down everything they say.

This evening, Berto didn't come home to dinner. The standards relax in his absence, and Jane and I ate sardines on toast in the kitchen. (With napkins, though.)

Afterwards, we shared a bath. It has been a habit of ours since I don't know when. She wanted me to have first go, when the water was hottest, since she prefers a cooler bath, but since my feet were sandy she agreed with my insistence on taking second turn. I told her where I had been and she said she hadn't been down to the beach yet this summer.

"Do you remember how I used to take you there every day when you were a child? You used to collect shells."

Like every other child. I used to make shell ladies, who carried baskets of cowries. Crinoline dresses of limpet on limpet. Painted topshells for the drawn-in waists and heavy busts. Orange, periwinkle heads and those thin, whorled shells for arms. There are still some dusty, broken ladies in my room in the attic. My memories of childhood here are far more vivid than my memories of childhood in Dublin.

Jane sounded wistful, as though she would like to recapture my childhood. Does she regret her lack of children? I can never ask. I never really thought of it before, but was I her child? Was that how she saw me? I don't think I ever regarded her as my mother.

Oh, but she annoyed me this evening. I have no time to sympathise with her thwarted instincts. I made the mistake of confiding in her. I suppose I felt vulnerable and close to her, because of Berto's absence and the fact that she and I were sharing the bath. Her hair was wispy and curled from the steam caught in the bathroom and the pink flush of her body as she dried herself made her look soft.

I told her I was writing a novel, and she laughed. And then she said that everyone of my age wanted to write a novel, and she laughed again at the thought of all those unwritten novels. When I asked her disdainfully had she ever wished to write a novel, she paused, with the towel held like a saw diagonally across her back, and she nodded her head. I was so cross and disbelieving that I was rude to her. I asked what on earth she could have written about?

"Exactly," she answered, and instead of being offended she roared with laughter again, so that I was left to feel that she might have put the same question to me. She then saw that I was hurt, and she apologised and said that mine might be different from all those others, but really, at twenty-one, one didn't know much.

"Sometimes, I think I know more than you."

"I know." Then she tied her hair back from her face, and daubed a yellow cream onto her skin so that she had obscene, oozing tear-drops on her cheeks. So long as I kept it as a hobby, she said. And didn't count on it to bring in the old lolly.

I didn't reply. I just left the bathroom, banging the door behind me, and I ran up the stairs to the attic with tears of rage dropping down my face. Now I am sitting on my bed in my nightdress, wondering what possessed me to tell her about the novel. She never even bothered to ask me what I might write about. For her there is nothing new under the sun. Everything is repetition. We all just head in the same direction in the same way. Nothing changes.

She came creeping up to my room after I had turned the light out and she tapped with fragile fingernails on my door.

"Lizard," she whispered. "Lizard. I didn't mean ..." But I lay mute as a fish and I heard her sigh and retreat. She hasn't learnt the vagaries of this last staircase and boards creaked abominably as she descended to her own floor.

Wednesday

I had no idea that they were so close to opening the craft shop. When Jane was talking about it that first night, the shop had sounded more imaginary than actual. Another of Berto's schemes. I suppose one becomes dismissive. But I was wrong. This is being managed by Jane, and by dint of worrying and fretting and working, she has been extraordinarily efficient. I didn't think she was capable. She has researched the whole business thoroughly and has been collecting stock all through the past winter.

"Come down to the Lodge with me," she said, the morning after we had fought in the bathroom. She and I were alone in the house. Mrs. Cleary's aunt had died and she was gone to the funeral. Berto had disappeared to see a man in Ennis. Something about aerial photographs. Berto is becoming dangerously excited again. Secretive too. He always becomes secretive when he is planning a new venture. He drops hints which he hopes you will take up. He is just like a child. I fear he is about to gamble again. A project which is really going to put him in the Big Time. Entice riches. I certainly don't encourage him to speculate. One hopes that if one seems disinterested, he will lose interest himself. Even Jane hasn't shown her usual, patient enthusiasm. I think she is delighted he has something else to occupy his energy while she continues to arrange her shop. She is proprietorial. It is strange that someone with so much latent business sense as Jane should not see through Berto. I think it is more that she refuses to look closely. She prefers to see Berto as successful. But I don't know that she can continue to pretend indefinitely.

To get back to that morning.

"I haven't shown you the stock yet."

I had been avoiding opportunities to see the stock. I had been refusing to be drawn into her enthusiasm, but I must admit I had been curious. I had looked inside the Lodge but hadn't gone further than those two front rooms.

She tucked her arm through mine as we walked down the drive.

"I didn't mean to hurt your feelings last night, Lizzie. I was being tactless. Things on my mind, I suppose."

Jane is as tall as myself. Not plump exactly, but she has what you might call a presence. She will make a good business woman. Someone to whom the general public might defer. She can adopt a poker face. But her face, looking closely at mine as we walked somewhat awkwardly down the uneven drive, arm in arm, did look concerned. For her injury to me? Worry about Berto? I couldn't tell.

"It didn't matter," I said, and though she must have known I was lying, she took the acceptance of apology at face value.

"This shop would give you marvellous experience for a novel," she said then, as we went into the Lodge. She nodded good morning to the three workmen, but didn't stop to speak with them. We clambered over half-sawn boards, wood peelings, cans of paint, unattached radiators.

"Will it really be ready in a month?" I asked doubtfully as we climbed the stairs.

"No. It will be ready in three weeks. It will be open in a month."

The staircase in the Lodge is narrow and dark and it winds round upon itself.

"We'll have quite a job getting the stock downstairs. You will help, won't you?"

"Mmm."

I could see what was happening. I was being drawn into this simply by my presence in the house. I could quite see that once the shop was open I could hardly exclude myself from the running of it. I could scarcely be churlish if Jane asked me to stand in while she is off somewhere for a day. I'll be forced to participate. But I do not want to be tied and I resent Jane's most obvious moves to interest me. Using the novel as a lure was a ploy which annoyed me.

"Think," she said blandly, as she unlocked the main bedroom door, where Berto's mother used to sleep before they had to bring her bed downstairs, "of all the conversation you would overhear." As though the writing of a novel involved snippets of conversation written down.

"A wonderful opportunity to observe people. It would be good for you to have a bit of responsibility."

I was saved the necessity of a reply because she opened the door and stood back to let me see the contents of the room. Most of the stock was still packed into boxes, but there were enough loose items for me to receive an initial impression of quality, and then she unpacked some of her particularly satisfactory pieces. She has decisive taste.

"What do you think?"

There were articles amongst the collection she showed me that I would not have been averse to housing myself, and I said so. There was no trash.

"Shouldn't you be catering to poor taste as well?" I asked, but she shook her head.

"People don't come to an exclusive shop, in an exclusive location, looking for rubbish."

Perhaps so. Even the tiny things were well made. There were some shell mice, and their tails were made from those very long, thin, whorled shells, three to a tail. There was something which linked each shell, but it was so carefully managed that I couldn't see what it was. I suppose the location *is* unique. I hadn't quite recognised the ambience.

"We should have a cheap souvenir shop down in the village. Then we would cover both ends of the market. But Berto won't agree and I don't like to go against his wishes. Berto says he doesn't see himself as a chain store operator. Can you imagine? Two souvenir shops and he talks of a chain. I was quite surprised when he refused. Usually the slightest idea fires him, but he's never been keen on shops. Even this shop irritates him."

Surely Berto wouldn't be against a shop simply because it was Jane's idea. I don't see Berto as petty in that way. No. I think the fact of the matter is that a shop is too simple a concept. Any fool, as far as Berto is concerned, could run a shop. He would prefer to succeed in something far more dashing. Berto is content enough for Jane to run the shop, but he doesn't wish to be curtailed himself by something so humdrum. No wonder she would like me to help out.

Jane's fingers, as she wrapped up the objects which she had taken out to show me, were worshipful.

I asked her why she hadn't started a shop before now, and she shrugged. She didn't know. She had, she supposed, spent a lot of time on the house. And Berto's mother. She had also spent a lot of time backing Berto.

"And are you going to stop backing him now? Is that it?"

"Certainly not." We were leaving the room, and I couldn't see her face as she bent over the key. "I simply won't have as much time to help Berto now."

Her face, when she finally straightened up, was flushed. "Besides, Berto doesn't need help from me. He is quite capable of running schemes on his own."

How to withdraw loyalty with loyalty. Out in the drive, she stretched, lifting her arms high above her head. "Isn't it a beautiful day?" Her face was speckled with sun. Jane has freckles. Bright lichens dotted over her nose and her cheekbones. Her hair is fading from blond to grey, but you would scarcely notice. She has what I call a permanent face. I wish I was not so fond of her. If I disliked her, I could leave without any commitment. But I am close to her. She can pretend as much belief as she wishes but I know that she is worried by Berto. She is desperate for her shop to be successful. She needs me as her shop assistant. It may be that Berto doesn't want to play shop. But it isn't possible to be sure, and she is worried. I know what she is trying to do. She is trying, stealthily, to cut Berto out from all participation in this shop. She wants it for herself. The money invested is hers and she feels personal ownership.

If she asked an outsider to help, without consulting Berto, he might just be hurt enough to insist on assisting himself. She doesn't think he wants to help, but she is afraid to ask him for fear he might say yes. I am the only one she can invite into the venture without upsetting Berto; indeed, with Berto's collusion, since it would all be under the guise of doing Lizzie good. I don't think it is that she doesn't trust Berto. It may just be that she would like to be in command and she can hardly be in command if Berto is helping. She may even believe him to be a carrier of bad luck. Jane believes in seventh sons of seventh sons and black cats and breaking mirrors.

But Jane can't divulge her thoughts to either Berto or myself. She can only say to Berto that she feels she should get me involved, for my own good. And to me, she can only say that I need to do something. She can't give her real reasons.

She is in a spot. So am I. I am the only person who can help her. I looked at the day and I looked at Jane and I said I thought I would go for a walk before lunch. She was hoping I would ask her to come with me, for nostalgia. But I extended no invitation and she turned back up the drive.

"Bye."

"Bye."

And we both turned around to wave at the same time.

The trouble is, I am so fond of Jane, and even my dislike of Berto has affectionate undertones. I can't help becoming enmeshed in and infected by their affairs. Nothing is ever straightforward. It was very well to think, in America, that when I came home I could hold myself aloof. To come here and to find the usual mess has inevitably confused plans. In the States, I could only think of how they might interfere with me with their concern and all the rest of it. I had forgotten how I used to get too caught up by *my* concern for *them.*

Thursday

The sun has reduced the colours of the mountains to nothing. They appear in the distance as no more than shivering clouds of smoke. The ploughed fields are dry and cracked and the soil, if you pick it up in your hands, is harsh and crumbles to gravel between the fingers. They say it will be a bad summer for tillage and already the hay is damned. Berto says they say that every year. He has fields around the rectory which he rents out to a neighbouring farmer, and the grass there is flowering without making leaf. But Berto doesn't know. I don't believe he realises that grass has flowers. Even in flower, the grass looks withered and scorched by the sun. When I was a child I used to run a stalk of grass, stacked full with seeds, through my teeth and all the seeds would be torn off into my mouth. I used to chew the seeds and then spit out the dross.

Walking along the road on my way to the beach today, I realised what I had been missing since my return. I have been lacking gaiety, riveting conversation. Friendly faces. I have not met a single, like-minded person (except Mick and he's too old) since my reaching here. I have been cloistered with that pillar of society, my cousin. Who told me this morning that she has never been inside one of the village pubs. And then she corrected herself. She once entered the one on the quay, to buy a bottle of Guinness to put into her Christmas pudding. It is not that she doesn't drink. She is not, as she so loftily said, a part of the pub culture.

This came up when I asked her was there any music going on in the town. After she had ascertained what it was that I meant by music (and we mean entirely different things) she admitted an ignorance. She advised me against the local pub life. I am unlikely to meet a nice type of person there.

I wish I had said nothing. Jane is now going to see if she can't get a bit of socialising going for me. So God knows what she will dredge up from her litter of suitable people. I feel it is incumbent on me to prepare an antidote. Mick says there is music in Donovan's on a Friday night, so tomorrow night I shall go on the town in my best faded jeans, looking, to put it baldly, for a fellow.

I'm afraid I am out of practice. I am also afraid that no one will look twice at me. Having lived so long with Rohan, I am back to my most panicky, seventeen year old fears of rejection. I can't remember how to chat with intent.

This morning I looked terribly carefully at myself in the long mirror in Jane and Berto's bedroom. I tried tying my hair back, and I tried leaving it loose and hanging. My hair most certainly looks fine. It still has lights in it from the desert and my skin is a darker gold than my hair. I am afraid, though, to expose myself. I felt safer when I had huffed breath on the mirror and could only see a hint of myself. I suppose I am insecure because Rohan so readily disposed of me. I can't be so indispensable as all that. The efficiency with which he returned me has ruined my confidence. I mean, he made financial arrangements with his father before consulting me. Then he told me I was going home. I knew we were breaking up, but I had thought, in so far as I allowed myself to think, that I would make my way to California and pick up some job there. But he said he didn't want to abandon me. He said he thought I was too young to abandon, but he knew I would resent his help, so he had just gone ahead and arranged my departure. He was not so concerned for my youth when he picked me up at eighteen. And of course, once I saw a way home, I was reluctant to refuse the opportunity. Besides, I was so used to following his lead.

Now I am nervous. Mick says that if he were ten years younger ... Even Berto is not unappreciative in a minor way. But in the time-honoured plea, I want someone to be interested in my mind. I have all sorts of fatuous hopes like that, but when I consider the vast, unfurnished expanses of my head, I think the hope is unmerited. I want to learn the centre of things. I am sick of following this rule or that rule, this category or that category. I want to know enough to make my own decisions without reference to someone else's conventions.

I have had to question myself to see if my refusal to work in the shop has been bloody-mindedness. Jane mentioned a salary yesterday, which would make possible my return to the States next summer. And it is an interesting job. Jane herself has said so many persuasive things and she is so enthusiastic. If I didn't know that she has her own interests in view more than mine. But then, who hasn't?

Put at its lowest. Perhaps I owe it to her. I mean, it is not as though she was my parent, and yet she cared for me as a child. She did, honestly, give me a feeling of being loved. Of being the centre of somebody's attention, in a way my father never did. I would feel no obligation were she my mother. I would reckon that all obligations had been equalized by now. But given the circumstances, I am cornered by my conscience.

I have agreed to look after the shop for the summer. It may be compromise. It may be weak-minded. But I really couldn't desert Jane. And it's so boring here. As she says, it could be a long summer with nothing at all to do and I do find I have been brooding about Rohan. The thing is, there is no one to whom I can talk about Rohan. I would love to find out where other people think I made mistakes. Or did we just disengage? I miss his skin. The smell of him. I miss being able to turn and say, Rohan, did I tell you? These are not things I can mention to Jane. Although, for the first time, Jane has allowed herself to admit that I have had a broken love affair. A serious one. She came up to my room, looking for me, last night, and discovered me lying out on my bed, crying, and when she rushed over to me asking what was wrong, what was the matter, had she said anything to make me upset, I could only roll my head to and fro on my pillow and sob out Rohan's name.

She went downstairs and came back up with the decanter of brandy and two glasses. And we sat on my bed, me with my eyes red and swollen, she with a perturbed look to her face, and we drank brandy together. But even then I couldn't really talk about Rohan to her. He is too remote from a person like Jane. Instead Jane talked. She said she had never had a broken love affair. Berto was the first and last man, and she looked as soft as a chicken. She really loves him. It is incredible, but she just adores him. Then she apologised to me. I'm not sure why. She said it twice. "I'm sorry, Lizard." I suppose she was apologising for being Jane and old-fashioned and disapproving and for underestimating my unhappiness.

She even went and got me a clean pillow case because mine was crushed and damp with tears.

Friday

This morning, when I was collecting the paper, Mick invited me out for a drink. Well, not invited me out exactly. He said why wouldn't I come down to Donovan's that night and he would buy me a drink. He knows I'm terrified to walk in there alone.

I couldn't resist telling Jane at lunch-time. I laid it on a bit too. I told her I had a date with Mick. Poor Jane. She spends her time trying to balance equality and social strata. She does not think Mick suitable, but she couldn't say so as she has a dread of being discovered to be a snob. She tightened her lips and withdrew into a quiet mood of self-reproach. From which she emerged over coffee to say that next week, yes, next week, she was going to have a little party in my honour. Really, she should have made arrangements long ago, but what with the shop and this and that, she had put it off. But she would make amends. Then she kissed me and apologised energetically for neglecting me and I felt very small. I tried to protest and say that I didn't feel in the least bit neglected and that she wasn't to dream of rustling up any sort of party, considering that the shop is to be opened so shortly. But she was not to be deflected.

What is more, she then took me to Limerick for the afternoon, and she bought me a dress as I have so few suitable clothes. The dress is actually beautiful, a thin but heavy material, a swathe of blending reds so that it looks shadowed by colours. And shoes. Very high-heeled sandals. We went to the best shop and spent a long time searching through waves of clothes on moving clothes rails. It is understood that the dress is to be kept for suitable occasions, and we both know what she means.

Oh, the dress *is* beautiful. It is a long time since I have worn a dress like this. I spent ages up in my bedroom before dinner trying it on. It wraps itself around my body. It caresses me. It does. I should have been helping Jane with dinner, I know, but instead I was standing in my room, wearing the dress as though it were the most intimate of lovers. Rohan has never seen me in a dress like this. I was thinking the most childish things, like, perhaps if I had worn such a dress, he would have asked me to stay. I know it was silly, but one gets the most ridiculous, the most pathetic hopes at times. I took it off before going downstairs and instead put on a clean pair of jeans. Jane says she can't tell the difference between my clean jeans and my dirty jeans, but then she doesn't wear them herself. She doesn't know how they tighten when they're clean. I also put on my blue, silky shirt. (It's nylon actually, but very thin and floppy.)

Berto was in a foul mood this evening. He had been over to Ennis, not once, but twice, during the day, and on neither occasion had he been able to see the man he was looking for. He has been expecting a phone call from this man since the weekend.

"Why don't you ring him?" asked Jane in her most

aggravatingly placating voice, and he nearly bit her head off.

"I don't have his phone number."

"Well, I'm sure he will ring, if he said he would."

"Hmm."

"What is he ringing about, anyway?"

"Photographs. He's taking some for me."

And Berto looked round at us both expectantly.

"What sort of ...?"

"Aerial. People's houses."

"Photographs?"

Jane looked shocked.

"Berto. That's spying. Are you sure it's legal to go flying about in the sky, photographing private property?"

"Prints. We enlarge them and we sell them, framed. Unusual view. You know. People like it. We'll even touch them up for a consideration."

Jane sighed and stared at the piece of potato speared on her fork, and as she stared, the pronged potato broke in two and both halves fell to her plate. With difficulty she caught up the smaller of the two halves and put it hurriedly into her mouth. Jane won't ever turn her fork over and use it as a scoop. Bad manners to do that. Given manners and efficiency, manners will always win. Berto, his mood improved by Jane's questions, refilled our glasses with wine.

"Grant, the other chap, was to go up in a Cessna, with a photographer, at the weekend and cover one of the Ordnance Survey grids."

"What do you mean, cover it?" I asked.

"The houses. Taking photographs of ..."

"Every single house? Before you even know if they want one?"

My questions were obviously infantile, and they

annoyed Berto.

"It is the actual picture. Their own home. In colour. They need to see it."

Jane nodded. "Oh indeed. In order to persuade them. And imagine seeing your house with the whole garden before and behind laid out in the same photograph. No. The scheme itself sounds frightfully good, Berto. Really it does. Quite one of your best. But this man, what did you say his name was? Grant? Who is he? I've never heard you mention the name before. Do we know him?"

"No. We don't know him."

Berto and Jane are entirely on the same wavelength. Berto recognises the nuances in the verb to know.

"English fellow. Bought the Rover from him. He's a pilot, turned mechanic. Buys in cars, a couple a week. Does them up and sells them. Like my Rover."

"Oh." Jane bit her lip. "Do you know anything about him, Berto?"

Berto banged his knuckles together with impatience. "Been dealing with him for weeks. Over the Rover first, and then over these photographs. He saw the possibilities immediately. Almost a step ahead of me all the way. Keen business sense, as well as being a first rate pilot." Berto took a long drink of wine, and shook his head gently in admiration of Grant. Berto adores macho men. Then he put his arms on the table and leaned forward towards Jane. "We formed a company last week and we hired a plane, which he was to take up on the Sunday if the weather was good."

Jane looked out the window as though by looking she could see back to Sunday. "Sunday. Oh yes. That was a beautiful day. Lizzie and I were weeding all afternoon. Don't you remember, Lizzie?"

I nodded, and then turned to Berto.

"Perhaps he has disappeared with the photographs.

Perhaps he'll try to sell them on his own."

"Nonsense."

"But if he was supposed to ring you the day before yesterday."

"He'll have had his reasons."

I said no more. I didn't suppose that the cost of hiring a plane and a photographer for one afternoon would amount to much. Jane obviously thought the same, because she smiled suddenly and touched Berto on the face. "I'm sure you're right, Berto. The phones are so awful these days. Anything might have happened."

Berto was irritated when I told him my plans for the evening. He came straight out with the fact that he did not think Mick was the right class. For once, I answered him back instead of remaining silently angry. I told him he was a disgusting snob, and that one thing I had learnt in the States was egalitarianism, at which, still smarting under my earlier perverse questioning, he became rather nasty.

"And look where your egalitarianism has led you."

"What do you mean?"

Tears began to sting my eyes. They always come when people are spiteful. He just looked at me.

"We both know what I mean, Lizzie," he said eventually. I raised my eyebrows. I wasn't able to speak, because I had one of those treacherous lumps of tears forming somewhere behind my throat and my nose.

"There are certain advantages," he said, "to being what you provocatively term snobbish, if being a snob means understanding where to draw the line."

Then he had the grace to look ashamed of himself, and Jane turned on him quite savagely. I have never heard Jane attack Berto before. She told him that she was embarrassed by him. She presumed, she said, that he must be feeling in very bad form, but she was not going to have her cousin spoken to in that way.

Then Berto turned on her and said it was all her fault, and why hadn't she arranged more entertainment for me instead of spending all her time fussing about the bloody shop. And what was Richard going to think if his daughter was allowed to swan around with every Tom, Dick and Harry in the village?

I couldn't stand it any more and I left the diningroom with as much dignity as I could in the hope that, with me out of the way, their fight would cease.

Later, when I heard them in the kitchen washing up, I crept guiltily down the stairway. They were still fighting. Over me, I supposed.

I didn't think that Berto would be so spiteful, though. I suppose that he is terribly conservative and he is rarely challenged. He is afraid that in some way my actions will make him laughable. He does not want to lose face with his neighbours. It is apparently one thing to be beyond the pale in the States. It is quite another to be conspicuous in Berto's house.

I hate scenes. I was so infected by his anger that I ran all the way down the drive, and my heart was pounding by the time I reached the gateway where the trees make feudal, blackened spears of shadow across the road.

And, after all that fuss, Mick never turned up. When I arrived at Donovan's there was a note left for me to say that a traveller from Dublin had called and Mick had taken him up to Galway for the evening.

Donovan's is a shop-cum-bar. The shop is a long, fusty, cement-floored passage, which finally bellies out into a bar. A passage grave, and the burial chamber is a bar where you can be buried, drink and rise again. It is small and dark and could provoke a perverse loyalty.

Mrs. Donovan, prim and restrained, with a bun pinned up by giant tortoiseshell pins, asked me, as though it were my social duty, what she could get me to drink. On Mick. He had apparently left instructions.

The note was written on lined paper, which caused me to lose confidence. If there is one thing I could be said to have a prejudice about, it is letters written on lined paper. I could almost feel Berto digging me in the ribs and hear him asking if I saw what he meant.

The family kitchen lies beyond the bar, and once, when the door was opened, I saw a tiny child rolling four empty bottles round the kitchen floor. A cracked dart board hangs down in the darkest section of the bar with a couple of rusted darts stuck into the bullseye. There were a few half-drunk youths of seventeen or so who snickered and nudged at my entrance. They were gathered apathetically round the pool table, while above their heads an omnipotent television flickered. There were drinkers, surrealistic under smoke, dispersed around the room, all silently watching a cowboy film.

There was no music. The fiddler was watching the film too. Mrs. Donovan didn't think he'd be playing until after eleven, if I wanted to wait.

I didn't stay long. It had been like stepping into a scene from the Depression. You know. Buddy, can you spare a dime? There was a moroseness which pervaded the dank, stained gloom, and I finished my drink as quickly as I could. Mrs. Donovan called me "Dear" with indifference, and she patted my hand when I pushed my glass across the counter. She said she'd tell Mick he would have been better letting the commercial traveller eff off for himself. "He's a terrible man for the work," she said. "He's forever at it."

Then her eyes slid past me to focus on the television and I walked out of the bar.

The street outside was sad. Dishevelled. With a scattering of disparate people. Five recalcitrant old men, lured and then neglected by the night, resentfully following their undelineated paths to oblivion. A guard watched them. He picked his nose while he waited for some activity. Two girls with tennis rackets. A woman, yawning behind her hand, a scarf over a crown of night rollers, walked a dog tediously from lamp post to lamp post. Success at the fifth, the eighth and the thirteenth. Harmony of thirds and fifths and home again, with a furtive nod to the exploring guard, who stood, a robust shadow, waiting for the pubs to close. Shop windows drew dim attention from the street lights and the names above were faded to pencilled obscurities. The town looked abandoned and lifeless. A netherworld of waiting, and I was glad to be beyond its edge in the undisturbed moonlight.

I do not like being stood up.

There wasn't a breath of wind tonight, and the thick silence was pierced intermittently with the bubbling, rising cries of curlews. It is odd that they should cry in the dark. It was still warm and I walked slowly along the road, reluctant to return to the house.

Mr. Grant had not telephoned in my absence. He had done better. He had arrived. With photographs. He was effusive with apologies when he heard how Berto had been trying to contact him for days. He'd been travelling. A job had come up. That, he said, was the way it went in his line of business. A good car came up for sale and you had to follow it up immediately. No time for delay. He should have left a message for Berto, but then again, they didn't want to be broadcasting their business, did they? The idea was up for grabs and their only way to corner the market was with secrecy. Not that he didn't trust the landlady, but you couldn't be sure of anyone these days.

When he had returned, he had obviously worked with great efficiency, for there were developed photographs spread out like cards on the walnut table in the drawing room. Jane was studying them with ebullient curiosity.

"Now where is that? Let me see. Oh yes. The Keaveneys. My goodness. Who would have thought that the back would look so derelict. When the front is so prim with its asters and lobelia and marigolds. And oh, look at this one. The doctor's house. That's splendid. Isn't it? Berto. Show Lizzie the Rectory."

It did look quite fine. Even on such a small print. The photographer had taken the Lodge into the same print, and the curve of the drive was shown by a canopy of leaf. The Lodge looked so secretive and evasive.

On the sofa was propped a huge, framed enlargement of a house. I don't know whose the house was, but it was framed by this perfectly dreadful mock gilt frame. Ornate and fiddly. Quite frightful.

"Gosh, how horrific," I said, before I could stop myself.

Berto looked annoyed. Not because his sentiments would have differed from mine, but because he and Jane were obviously being cautious in their comments for fear of wounding the personal susceptibilities of Mr. Grant. They suspected him of being a devotee of the gilt-edged frame, and were themselves at a loss for words. But Mr. Grant smiled and moved in front of me, brushing my arm, deliberately I'm sure.

"I agree, Miss, eh?"

"Lizzie."

"Lizzie. I agree. I wouldn't dream of offering the gilt frame in this house, for instance. I mean, you have to gauge your customers. You know. The decor and all the rest. For you, I would produce this."

He removed the first frame, and behind there was a smaller, plain black frame, surrounding the same house. Even the print was different. A matt finish. Jane had moved forward.

"Oh that's very nice. Most pleasant. Don't you think so, Berto?"

The relief in her voice was marked. Mr. Grant smiled and stood there in front of me. "Well, Lizzie?" he asked, trying to hold my eyes. "Are you impressed?" I shrugged, annoyed, and looked away. I walked over to the walnut table to look once more at the photographs.

"They're very pleasant for an album, I suppose. But I can't imagine people buying those huge ones. I mean, what's the point unlesss you're moving away and you want some remembrance?"

"You'd be surprised. A photograph like that adds to the sense of permanence. Adds a touch of solidity."

Berto, his voice sounding light now, and teasing, said, "She's very young in the business sense."

I could have killed him. I didn't look at anybody, but began to shuffle the photographs around on the table. I could feel Mr. Grant look at me again. I could imagine his smile. I knew damn well what he was thinking.

Jane said she thought we had some whiskey in the house. "Why don't you have one with us, Mr. Grant, before you go?"

He thanked her, and while Berto disappeared to fetch the whiskey, he took out a packet of cigarettes and offered one to both of us. Jane accepted, and then he shook one out for himself, tapped it on the box, put it in his mouth and lit it. Then he lit Jane's. He nodded towards me. "I'd say that suntan's not out of a bottle. Have you been on the continent?"

"Lizzie's recently come home from America," Jane said

"Quite a change, I'd say."

I nodded.

"You'd find the pace pretty slow after ..."

"Surely you don't go to this much trouble for each photograph?" I pointed to the framed photograph, but he took my meaning.

"Of course not." And then with a glance to Jane, to include her, he became technical again. "We show them from one sample what they could have. There are nice touches. Gradations of price. This one, for instance," and he touched the black frame, "is mounted on canvas. You pay for that. And if you don't want unsightly sheds, or the septic tank, to be included in the photograph, we can touch them out artistically. You pay for that too. The prices go as low as thirty pounds, but nothing less than that. They have to think they're buying something special. Put the prices any lower and they'll be suspicious."

"So you and Berto will be selling door to door? Somehow I can't imagine Berto in the role, but ..."

"Initially, Lizzie. Initially." Berto had come back in. "We build the business up ourselves and then we turn the legwork over to someone else. We see the venture becoming nationwide."

"Mr. Grant has done awfully well already, Lizzie." Jane put down the small group of photographs she still held in her hand. "He has taken something like twenty orders already. It's marvellous in such a short time."

Jane's voice demanded praise. She was clearly still recovering from her row with Berto and she was damned if I was going to stir up anything else. I saw her point. I couldn't decide whether her enthusiasm for the photographs was faked or genuine. With Jane, it can be impossible to tell.

I did not like Mr. Grant myself, but I think that Jane

was impressed by his efficiency. I must admit I was impressed myself, and as for Berto, I think he was almost overwhelmed by the speed at which things had been moving without his knowledge. I wondered did he feel slightly by-passed. My own reason for disliking Mr. Grant was perfectly simple. He fancied me and I most emphatically did not fancy him, but his presence made me acutely aware of my body as I have not been aware of it since my departure from the States. I decided to leave them to their whiskey.

"I think I'm going to bed," I said, and then I could have bitten my tongue off. He has one of those open-pored faces. Dark eyes. Dark hair. Erroneously regarded as handsome. He said, without smiling, and before Jane or Berto had time to say a word, that he hoped I would sleep well, but he thought that the night might prove rather too hot.

He was right. I was disturbed. I couldn't even undress until I heard his car driving away half an hour later. While he was still present in the house, I could imagine him watching me. Later I was undressing and watching myself in the mirror. I was a stripper by choice. Wishing that someone would watch. I remembered undressing in the motel room that last morning in New York, and thinking that this was the last time Rohan would ever see my body and the bastard never bothered to look around from the early morning television. He said afterwards that he had been waiting for a weather report to know what sort of flight I was due to have.

Slept restlessly.

Saturday

I lay in bed all morning, even though I could see that the sun was shining. Berto spent the morning circling the front lawn, seated on his small, tractor-like machine, cutting the grass, and the noise of the engine droning up to the attic was quite restful.

Over lunch he said he planned to circle the tennis court and its perimeters during the afternoon, and afterwards, perhaps I would help him to mark the lines. He was dressed in his old clothes. Corduroy trousers, green stained at the knees from where he had been kneeling by his lawn-mower, praying to it to start. A jersey with leather patches on the elbows and small holes gathered like mouths around the edges of the patches. Berto looks at his best dressed like this. Defenceless and uncorrupted. Berto in such attire draws affection. It is at times like this that one realises that he is totally self-deceived. He sees himself as successful, hard-working and interesting. Not laughable. Not sad. Not suspect. Not gullible. He does raise in one the desire to protect. After all, Berto is a happy person. He may not be deep-thinking. He may be prejudiced. He may have annoying habits. But he is content. And there are so few contented persons about, it would seem criminal to disrupt his contentment. It's not as though he's harmful. There isn't anything criminal about being a failure, and so surely it is churlish to want him to see himself as a failure, to recognise his faults. Because if Berto was to see himself as a failure, I'm sure he would be absolutely punctured. Quite defeated. He would never be able to analyse where it was that he had gone wrong. He would just be a failure and that would be that. No more Berto.

So when he started talking about Nick Grant at lunch time, I did nothing to quench his enthusiasm. Being Berto, he had forgotten his volatile rudeness to me on the previous evening and said no more about it. Instead he told me that Nick Grant had wondered if I would like to fly with him some time? "Said he thought you needed taking out of yourself a bit."

I only smiled. I couldn't bring myself to speak.

When I think of weekends in country houses, despite the fact that I have been coming here for years, I have erroneous ideas of what should happen. Fishing. Shooting. That sort of thing, with people stalking through the house in wellington boots, and gun-dogs farting in the hall. Berto and Jane don't know how to handle the country. Berto is nervous of the countryside. Bulls and things in every field. He has some beef cattle, but I don't believe he would recognise them if he saw them. A man looks after them, by some convoluted arrangement, which probably ensures a minimum of profit for Berto. I don't believe Berto has ever spent a day walking in the hills, and he only goes to sea in other people's speed boats. He can't identify the simplest of flowers and he doesn't even know enough about birds to shoot them. He hasn't really any hobbies. The awful thing is that he lives for these dreadful schemes of his.

This is what makes each new scheme so terrifying. There is always the fear that this scheme is going to be the one that unveils Berto to himself.

I think Berto imagines the world to be inhabited by what he calls decent people. He is never suspicious. Jane has been very taken by Grant. He fixed the brake linings in her car last night. She now thinks he is delightful.

When we were down at the Lodge, painting behind the new shelving, I asked her had she really liked him, and she said, oh yes. Without a hesitation.

"And what's more, he seems to know exactly what he's doing. Such a relief, because I must admit when Berto told me about him, I was worried. I mean, it all seemed so out of the blue and Berto does get carried away sometimes."

"And you trust Grant?"

"Nick. He did say to call him Nick. Absolutely. Did you like him?"

"Hmm."

"Really Lizzie, you *are* difficult. I mean, he might not be quite our cup of tea, but I would have thought that you, at least, would have been more gregarious than that. After all your preaching to poor Berto about equality."

"Nothing to do with equality. And I didn't say I didn't like him. I merely said hmm."

"It's awfully kind of him to offer to take you up in the plane with him."

Sometimes I wonder about the depths of Jane's naivety.

"Can you see Berto selling those gilt-edged monstrosities?"

"Certainly. He'll have great fun." Her tongue came out between her teeth as she jabbed with the tip of her paintbrush down to the edge of the shelving. "I do wish they'd left the shelving until after we had painted this wall. So short-sighted. My own fault for not coming down here yesterday."

This time she doesn't want to be involved with Berto's enterprise. She wants to remain aloof from the whole thing. She doesn't want to worry about him, so she is going to find Nick Grant nothing less than splendid. I can't blame her. For the first time since I have known Jane she is acting entirely in her own interests.

The shop is to open on a Saturday. Three weeks from today. While we painted, Jane suddenly conceived of an opening night for the shop and a drinks party actually in the Lodge. She became most excited by the idea.

"Like a preview," she said.

I muttered that I hoped she would be able to chain everything down.

"Oh Lizzie." She balanced her paintbrush on the lid of the opened tin and pushed her headscarf back from her forehead. Silk is so slippery. Who but Jane would protect her hair from paint splashes with a silk scarf?

"You're too cynical," she said. "I'm asking only friends. I'm not asking anyone like that."

"They're all like that, Janey darling." But I laughed.

"We could have it on the Thursday evening, clear up on the Friday and open on the Saturday."

The first of her series of advertisements is to appear in all the national newspapers on Monday. It is quite fun being drawn into all this, but I shall be glad when the summer is over. Buying and selling is not my aim in life. Enough to live on. I was thinking last night that I have never lived alone. I have never lived in a place by myself with only myself to please. I wondered if living alone would make me more or less dependent on other people.

Back at the house, Jane spent a long time on the

telephone, arranging the party. Just a small affair, six-thirty to eight-thirty. For the opening of the shop, you know. Oh, didn't I tell you? I thought I'd told simply everybody. Nothing special. Just a few friends. And my little cousin is home from the States. Do you remember her? Dying to meet some people. So lonely when you've been away for a while. Out of touch with all her friends, poor darling. Quite honestly at a loss. How lovely. We do look forward to seeing ...

After dinner, Berto and I mixed the lime and we marked out the lines of the court. A tedious job because the wheel which paints the lime kept jamming with bits of cut grass and drying lime. Still, we completed the task without too many wobbles and then, since the court looked tempting, we knocked up for half an hour. I'll say this for Berto. He is a good tennis player, and he taught me how to play. I remember kindly the patience with which he taught me. Hours spent down on the court, hitting balls to my backhand. Perfecting overspins and underspins. He even taught me strategy. But I can't beat Berto at tennis. I can give him a good match but I have never been able to win. Tennis is an area in which Berto doesn't compromise. He doesn't give away points.

Afterwards, not wanting to leave a white trail over the grass, we had to carry the court marker back to the basement, and as we were putting it away I noticed a collection of cardboard boxes in what used to be the scullery. The sort of room in which rabbits were skinned and the shot was hacked out of pheasants.

"Oh, I wonder if that is some stock which Jane has forgotten," I said, and I went over to one of the boxes and lifted up the lid.

"No."

Berto gave me a discomfited smile, and then shrugged,

put his hand down under mine and pulled something out of the box which I had begun to open. It was a mug. Plain white, apart from a transfer of the Pope on one side.

"Would you like one?" He proffered it to me. "I have five hundred. The Pope's visit. Souvenir mugs. Couldn't get hold of anyone to distribute them and I was a bit tied up myself at the time."

I hadn't taken the mug from him, and after dangling it to and fro from his finger for a while, he put it back in the box.

"Tried to persuade Jane to buy them from me for her shop, but she refused. Said they were the wrong tone and out of date."

"Bring them to Knock," I said and I swear his face brightened.

Their existence is so light and frothy and busy. They never stop moving. It makes one think there is nothing deeper to life. I wonder what they would do should anything ever go seriously wrong.

Sunday

The weather changed. When I woke up my face was cold and an abrasive wind blew through the open window.

Heavy rain stabbed and spat at the windows while we sat in the traitorous chill of the dining room, eating breakfast. The wind was making a hollow noise in the empty chimney. Jane said how wonderful for the garden.

I thought of those bloody lines on the tennis court being washed away and how we would have to paint them again during the week.

Berto was jagged with frustration. The Cessna was supposed to fly today and the photographer was to cover the second grid. The aeroplane can only be hired on a Sunday, and all through the week the weather has been superb but useless.

"How is one supposed to cope with this foul climate?"

He complained about the temperature of the coffee, about the economic climate of the country, about lack of back-bone, laziness, the IRA. He covered most areas. "This blighted, strike-ridden little country."

Jane suggested church, and he disappeared, enraged,

to put on a suit.

"We've just time to catch the eleven o'clock, if we rush," she said hopefully to me, but I shook my head.

"I'll tidy up here."

She was disappointed and to pay me back she suddenly said, "Well, you can do this much for me. You can come with me to visit the potter, what's-his-name. We'll go together after lunch."

I was amused at how she contrived to put me on the spot. Since I wouldn't go to church, then I could jolly well do this ... one of her best tactics. In fact, I have been wanting to meet him, so the hardship is all hers. I agreed charmingly to go with her, which made her hesitate.

"Are you sure?"

I expect she would like to have put off the visit indefinitely, so nervous does this man make her. I nodded.

"Indeed."

She looked at me uncertainly, and then she remembered that there was Holy Communion and it had been so long and she must hurry Berto up. She departed with her gloves and her hat and her bag, rushing with Berto from the front door through the spearing, vindictive drops of rain to the garage where the Rover is stabled in equestrian pretence. I heard it whinny several times with cold reluctance before it sidled out into the weather.

While they were at church, I did something which other people might consider odd. I went down to the Lodge and made myself a cup of coffee in the kitchen behind the shop. Playing house, I suppose. I collected my notebook from my bedroom, and I ran down the drive.

There were recalcitrant pools of sepia-tinted water in all the hollows on the drive. The ground accepted nothing. Descending rain had churned up the meanest layer of dust and spread wide traps of water. I took a dancing, erratic course down to the Lodge, and by the time I reached the door, the legs of my jeans, below the line of my jacket, were soaked, and one of those horrible channels of water was draining from my hood in under my chin.

I used to play in the Lodge as a child. When it was empty and unrepaired. Jane would give me a picnic and I would take it down the drive and set up living quarters for myself. She even gave me a rug and a pillow to keep down there for the summer, so that I could make a bed in one of the bedrooms, and I would play solemn games. It had been the home of the coachman, and there had been books belonging to him still lying damp and mouldy, their pages stuck together, on one of the upstairs floors. He, too, had been a religious man, for the books were, without exception, on church matters. I know, because I searched each one in the hope of finding a children's book or some exciting adult book. Those books were unrelievedly dull.

Later the house was repaired, the books burnt, and Berto's mother moved in. To my chagrin and also to the better-concealed chagrin of Berto and Jane. She was a difficult woman, touchy and self-centred. Her difficulties were compounded by severe loss of memory. Her furniture was the most important thing in her life, and she assumed its importance was equal for others. She threatened people with her furniture. Or she cajoled them with it. You can have this and this when I'm gone. Or not, if the mood took her. She came from a village in Wicklow, and Berto, who is not really given to cattiness, said that probably her friends threw a party after her departure. She never managed to work out who I was. She mostly thought that I was a maid, and used to tell me that I had surprisingly nice legs. She died suddenly of a heart attack, three years ago, which was when the shop must first have germinated.

I had intended to write this morning. I'm not just imagining I can write. Once, in the States, I wrote two short stories and I showed them to a woman we both knew well. A real writer. She said they showed distinct promise, and she was not a woman to raise false hopes. She said my observation was acute. But I needed more experience, more maturity. The main thing, she said, was to keep writing and to keep growing up. Which at the time sounded a bit fatuous. I felt so old in those days. But now I know what she means. I have been writing here. I have been making notes on all the people I know. I have almost an entire notebook on all that I remember of Jane and Berto. I didn't realise how much I knew about them. I have now extended the exercise and I am writing about Rohan and our relationship.

It is funny how Jane thinks that I used to be amenable, and yet I never felt amenable. I used to pretend a great deal. I think I still do. Maybe everybody poses. What am I posing as, I wonder? Sometimes I think I'm not so much posing as protecting myself. Secretive shells of this and that. I don't mean to pose. If it was possible, I should like to be seen as myself. Great, wonderful things like that. But I know that Jane wouldn't approve of my real self, and I am afraid to be exposed to her. So I pose as kind, concerned and useful. Because I like her to think well of me. After all, I have a long history of wishing Jane to think well of me. It is not surprising that I should still wish her to do so. Therefore I am about to do something for her which I don't want to do. Which is not part of my own programme of self-discovery. Perhaps I am also posing as a discarded lover. Rohan used to say that I was a dramatist. But impose was the word he used. I imposed on him.

I have to discount a lot of things said by Rohan in those last six months. He was trying to hurt me. I wasn't well then. His behaviour destroyed me. I couldn't eat and I couldn't sleep and I couldn't concentrate. The thought of how he treated me and the thought of how I clung. I'm sure it was cruel that he nurtured my dependence on him and then grew angry when I continued to depend after he had grown bored. I couldn't bring myself to leave his apartment. Couldn't believe it was finished. He used to tell me my tenacity was boring. What he did was not my business. At the beginning, he would tell me everything and I couldn't ask enough questions to satisfy him. The way it is with lovers. Minute details of the other person are intriguing. But then I continued to ask questions after he had regained the independence of no longer being in love, and the more loving my attention, the more it irked, because my continued love made him feel guilty and he grew cruel in self-defence. He said I was immature in my reliance on others. I needed, he said, to build up my self-respect, instead of relying on the respect of other people for me. Nasty maybe, but what else was he to do?

I wish I could imagine that he misses me. It would give me some satisfaction. But I imagine he feels only relief.

I don't only miss Rohan. I miss the States. I didn't feel middle-class in the States.

By the time I had come out again, the rain was flirting with the sun, spraying rainbows of fanned colours between the fields and the mountains. Possessive arcs of colour enclosed portions of landscape, framed them and intensified them. I saw, within the defined half-circles, the wet, stony hills glossed temporarily by the sun. Drowning, yellow fields were also encapsulated.

I am saying this because my moods are affected by the sun, and just walking back to the house, with the sun glinting and the clouds breaking, cheered me up immensely.

I would go so far as to say that Jane and Berto seemed refreshed by church.

Berto had also been affected by the change in the weather. It meant that the plane could fly in the afternoon. He had been invited to join the flight and he was both excited and nervous. Jane wouldn't let him have a second drink before lunch. Why, I'm not sure. Some idea of a sober jump to safety. Perhaps she was afraid he might be sick.

Jane lives in a dream. A fantasy. My God, imagine creating a fantasy out of Berto. It must take so much energy to believe in Berto. Today she was depressed. By Berto and his endless plans. His ups and downs. By the risks she is taking in opening yet another craft shop. Someone from Bórd Fáilte had come down last week and he had been very pessimistic about her chances of success. He had reminded her that we were in the middle of a recession, and he had questioned whether she quite understood the implications. There were shops going to the wall every day. Due to mismanagement, overstocking, lack of commitment and the general state of the economy. At the time, Jane had been raised to a state of adrenalin-assisted euphoria merely by arguing with him and having him cede several points to her. But today, in retrospect, she was ceding points to him. She still has the haunting suspicion that men know best.

This afternoon, certainly, she was being tormented by self-doubts. Partly brought on by the impending visit to the potter.

We walked, and on our way round the harbour she said, unexpectedly, that she believed in an afterlife.

"It couldn't be just this," she said, "and then nothing."

Poor Jane.

I wish I had gone to see Dylan on my own. Jane can be so embarrassingly effusive when she is unsure of herself. She uses the most unappealing forms of self-protection. Jane means well, and she's as kind as could be, but how can one explain that to outsiders when she is there and gushing abominably. At least my presence subdued the effect of her enthusiasm. With me there, Dylan must have seen the funny side of Jane (maybe even glimpsed the underlying kindness) instead of being merely irritated. Jane did say afterwards that she thought his manner much improved. He had smiled at her twice, and had smiled to himself several times, and she didn't care if he had been smiling at her expense. Why, she had seen *me* smile in complicity with Dylan at one point, and that didn't bother her at all. Did she talk too much?

I would prefer to have gone alone.

A steep boreen leads up to the cottage. There is a road round to the back of the house, but from the harbour it can more easily be reached on foot by the boreen. Idyllic place. The brambles grow up very tall on either side of the boreen, and long, bending summer shoots arch over the path. He will have to cut himself out before winter comes. Potatoes and cabbages I recognised in the plot of earth. Parsley by the door. An orange cat crouched by the wall. The cottage itself, squat, small-eyed under thatch. Too perfect. With the sun shining and the water below in the harbour mobile with drifting, flickering ripples, I suspected the authenticity of the place.

I remember Jane hoping that perhaps he might be out as she knocked on the door.

He was at home.

Things do not live in my hands. His pottery cats did

not purr when I stroked their glazed fur with my fingers. I am not saying that I did not find them beautiful. I am simply saying that I do not imagine life in objects. It is a difference between Jane and myself. It may be a disability in me that I do not possess that sort of imagination. It is her imagination which allows her to believe in an afterlife and I myself would like to be able to close my eyes and fly to eternity. But I can't and that is all there is to it. And all the while I was looking at the birds and the animals and thinking that I wished they would do for me what they did for Jane, Jane was saying all the sorts of mortifying things that Jane does say when she is ruffled ... my cousin's awfully interested in pottery, and she was simply dying to see your work ... back from the States after a rather difficult time (in lowered tones while I was stroking one of the real cats which lay somnolent in a chair) ... so nice for her to meet someone of her own age, and you know, she's quite artistic herself. She writes ... so nice for her to meet you because really it's frightfully lonely for young people like yourselves ... a little party ... why don't you come?

There was a hawk, which hovered, suspended by wire from the ceiling, and I wished that it would swoop down and pluck out Jane's tongue. The only thing I can say is that both Dylan and myself were silent, and our very silence was allegiance.

The cottage is more picturesque from the outside. Within, it is dark. The door is low and you have to bend your head to enter and depart, which emphasises the enclosed feeling of the interior. The sun only pokes narrow strips of light through the windows and I found the place depressing, lightened only by the countless birds and animals. The atmosphere of the room makes me think of dreary diseases like galloping consumption and the worst sorts of mental illnesses.

Dylan grudgingly promised Jane about ten pieces. At prices to be arranged. She is to collect them in the car during the week. But the negotiations put her further out of sorts. It is not that he is deliberately rude to her. It is just that their views are so much at variance, they could not be at peace with one another. He resents her. He knows he has to sell some of his stuff and he bitterly resents the buyers. He feels that they invade his privacy. Poor Jane. I suppose the tendency is always to despise the middleman in any negotiations. She was thoroughly aggravated by him. She finds him most unreasonable. Almost petulant. "Anyone would have thought he was doing me a favour by selling me some of his pieces. Really, he's quite impossible. Don't you think, Lizzie? I mean, when I'm so obviously doing him the favour. He's not going to find many buyers prepared to cajole his pottery away from him. What does he expect to live on?"

"But if he doesn't want to sell them, you can hardly be doing him a favour by wheedling them away."

I must say, I thought that most artists were frantic to sell their work. We knew some painters round Tucson, and a sale was a cause for celebration. Most of the painters we knew were pretty unsuccessful. Too many of them were doing the same sort of thing. Not enough individuality. And if one of them made a sale, the others all immediately copied whatever it was that had been sold and ruined the market.

The tide was out when we had climbed back down to the pier and some of the boats were stranded. The smell from the seaweed and the mud was disgusting and we hurried out of the village. The trouble is that Jane thinks the end of creating something is its sale. Whereas he thinks creation is the final point. He must have other sources of money to be able to maintain such a disdainful attitude. Jane said, as we were walking up the village street, that surely he wished to give pleasure to others. She was in a very mawkish humour today. Her churchgoing and her self-doubts must have made her simplistic in her views. If a man has five talents, he should make them ten ...

Berto pulled up behind us, hooting repeatedly, when we were almost level with the Cistercian Abbey. He was exhilarated both by the flight itself and by relief that it was safely over and that he would not be required to fly again. He had been up for half an hour before the arrival of the photographer. "The others will be flying until the light goes." Sitting behind Berto, I noticed that his ears were pink-tinged and that there was a roll of skin which caught loosely on the collar of his shirt. His hair is quite thin and is growing very grey. Jane has a pouch of flesh beneath her chin and when she turned her head towards Berto, the skin above her jaw wrinkled. I am emotional these days, and the sight of them both brought tears to my eyes. They looked so desiccated.

"Where did you go this afternoon?" Berto asked eventually, when he had told Jane all he could possibly tell her of his own activities. It had occurred to him that we must have been coming back from somewhere. Jane told him about Dylan. "So much gentler today. Lizzie charmed him like a bird. He has promised me some pieces. And he's going to come to my party. Just to see Lizzie, I'm sure. He was watching her all the time we were there."

"Oh Jane. For heaven's sake."

She has always been like that. She likes to boost one up, and she always does so in the most unconvincing of ways.

I must say, I was surprised that he had accepted her

invitation to the party. I would have expected him to refuse on grounds such as exploitation of the artist by the patron. The idea that Jane might wish to use him for display. A real, breathing artist.

I had forgotten how aggravatingly conceited Berto could become when business was going well for him. Now that he has his own project, he is inclined to be somewhat patronising about the shop. He talks of it with condescension in the intervals between talking of his own affairs.

They were somewhat chilly towards one another this evening, because Jane took umbrage at his attitude. At one stage she very pointedly took out her file of accounts and asked him if he could be quiet as she needed to work.

Monday

I still find it difficult to sleep at nights. It is at night that I seem at my emptiest. During the day I can be lulled into enjoyment of Jane's life. But at night-time I am honest and I find that the last few weeks have been wasted. This summer, I am riding on Jane's back and I am disgusted with myself. I suppose I need someone with whom I could talk. The way I used to talk to Rohan. Before he turned sour. Before he became the person who said, uh-huh, uh-huh, uh-huh, and looked long-eyed out the window and picked his teeth while I spoke.

It is at night-time that I wonder what he is doing and who he is with. Maybe he is with no one. Rohan, with his shirt picking up sweat from every crease in his belly, is at his worst round this time of the year. The approach of summer. He gets trapped into a somnolent hatred of the heat and he sits in the apartment for weeks, lethargic as a slug, and mean. I used to say, why not go up to the mountains and camp by a reservoir, the same as other people, but he'd only raise his eye-lids (and even that activated sweat) and shake his head. Nuh-huh, nuh-huh. Maybe he's different this year. Perhaps he is the way he was that first summer when he would go anywhere and do anything if it was to please me.

I checked myself in the mirror this morning, and I still look self-contained. I look fine really, but at breakfast Jane said she thought I looked peaky. I have circles under my eyes, she says, and she suggested that I should go for a walk. A nice, long walk. That has always been Jane's remedy.

Berto was drifting through the hall as I went out.

"Wouldn't like to come with me, would you?"

"Where?" I asked cautiously. Berto is always trying to wheedle promises out of people before he parts with the facts.

"Oh. Selling a few photographs."

I shook my head. "Certainly not." I looked at him curiously. "I am surprised you agreed to be the salesman, Berto. I didn't think that was your line of country at all."

"This is different."

"Oh? In what way?"

I know I shouldn't corner Berto, but really he has been rather insufferable, and now that he is dressing in suits and ties and black polished shoes he no longer looks pathetic.

"Fact is, Grant says he can't be expected to do everything. And I quite agree." He looked at me belligerently. "And I thought that since you obviously have nothing better to do, you might have been willing to help me. I mean ..." and he opened his hands in a gesture of generosity, and then closed them again to imply that his generosity in having me here and so forth was unreciprocated by me. Not that he said anything, but I know Berto and his gestures and his ways of using people and making them feel small.

"Sorry Berto. Jane says I look peaky. I am to go for

a good, long walk. Travelling in a car would be the last thing."

He went, shaking his head, into the cloakroom to fetch a hat.

I'm sure Berto considers it beneath his dignity to go from door-to-door in his own district, flogging framed photographs. I don't imagine, when he first ventured the scheme, that he had himself in mind for the leg-work.

There was a mist this morning. A light, gossamer heat haze which gave the impression that everything had been created from pin-pricks of colour. The morning was hollow with silence and the birds still had an early confidence, a brief tameness. A pair of tiny, burnished goldcrests clung to the Lodge wall above a window, pecking insects out of the pebble dash, and they were undisturbed by my quiet passing.

Berto does not notice birds. I don't believe he even hears birdsong. He is not attuned.

I am such a lazy person. I think of people these days. I never contemplate ideas. I have none. There are no books to speak of in the house and I have read nothing here. Jane never reads. Berto reads intermittently. Detective stories and manuals on how to do this or that. All I have been doing since I have come home is pretending to write. And then, this morning, I walked to the beach and sat on the grey sand and stared at the silky sea without writing a thing. I was impatient with myself and finally stood up, brushed the sand off my jeans and walked far round the point to where the lagoon joins the real sea. Beyond where people come. Out beyond the lagoon the sand stops and the beach is formed by rounded stones and crushed shells. Under the cliffs, great boulders have been thrown by the high tides, but I walked close to the water where the stones are tiny and they rustle underfoot.

The noise of the stones shifting at the edge of the tide reminded me of the time Rohan and myself did camp by a reservoir. The first summer. One of those chiselled times. A time to remain obdurately in the memory long after you might wish it to be eradicated. One of those floating, unattached periods, unrelated to any other period of one's existence. A time when no one else mattered. No one else came to mind. I have memories of Rohan's hair tangled up in mine and how, when we made love, we could hear the rush of tiny pebbles being ingested by the overturning ripples at the edge of the reservoir.

Rohan is still poignantly in my mind though there are times when I attempt to hate him.

The longer one remains in the Rectory, the more difficult it is to leave. I have become a part of the routine. Their influence is insidious. They so much expect me to be like them. Not even expect. They assume. Jane said last night, "We get on so well together, don't we?" But that is because she is getting her own way all the time. I have deferred to her or I have remained silent on so many things. There are points on which I can't be bothered to argue, because I know my arguments will get nowhere. Jane is not open to argument and change. Her views, for instance, on the working classes, are obsolete. As are her views on morality (and there is only sexual morality in Ireland). She still thinks that a baby born out of wedlock is a social disaster to the mother. She actually said to me the other night in a flurry of embarrassed confidence that she was glad that nothing awful had happened to me while I was in the States. Well, so am I. But our reasons differ. Jane is full of assumptions, which, if she ever bothered to analyse them, are no more than prejudices. She is so concerned with her public image. The look of things. I remember once how Rohan had been reading something about the German concentration camps. According to which, it was the German middle class which collapsed most dramatically under the SS. Because, he said, triumphantly, they had no ideals, religious or political, and they had no internalised morality. So there you are, you see, he had said on that occasion, with a nod of his head as though everything had been proved beyond doubt. He had been throwing the middle class mantle over me at the time. He was right. Still is to some extent. But I'm struggling to escape. Jane, though, is middle class to the core. This matter of form is tremendously important to her. It transcends everything else. Knowledge, Rohan would say, is your only protection, when he would come home to find that I had idled away another day, listening to records, walking around town, waiting for him to come home. Unhealthy, I know. I existed almost at second hand. Through him. I thought that it was enough to be in love. A fulfilling activity in itself. No wonder I palled. Everything that I did was sporadic, unsustained. Even my writing was sporadic. I would write something, have it rejected and I would stop writing.

I am afraid that I am falling back into the middle class trap before I have properly escaped.

Rohan frequently accused me of being childish. My childishness ended by disgusting him. He saw it as a deliberate flaw. An excuse for not being anything. For laziness. My dependence on him, for instance. What right had I to imagine I could depend on him? Legally I was not allowed to work in the States. I had an excuse for idleness. But for him that was not good enough. Other people worked illegally, why not me? Instead, I wasted myself quite contentedly. The argument, and it was a big argument in that final period, was exacerbated by the fact that he was trying to suppress guilt. Because at the beginning it had been Rohan who had persuaded me to stay in America. He had not been concerned about my infantile mind in those days. Isn't it one of the most frightening things which a man can attempt to do to a woman? He can play on her childishness, invest her dependence with glamour, the way Rohan did in the first two years. It was only when he had grown apart from me and wanted to be rid of me that he became so militant. And partly out of spite, partly out of fear, I resisted all his efforts to make me independent. His campaign was too expedient.

It was ironic that when I came home at lunch time there should have been a letter from Rohan. He says he hopes we can still be friends. The whole letter was like that. Pointless. I mean, once we had ceased to be lovers, how could he dare to attempt a bland friendship? And at such a distance. He tells me he has started jogging. Why the hell should I want to know? The information is of no value to me. He has even joined a club in order to give himself the competition. They run at quite a high altitude. Adidas. Split-timing. Jock straps. Nothing about women. Nothing that really matters. Damn him.

I despise myself really. I want to belittle him. I even want to dislike him. They say it is a period one goes through after one has finished an affair. And I never believed them. I always thought I would be rather grand and forgiving and altogether admirable. Instead I find that I am like all those others. Vindictive.

Perhaps I should write to him. Something cutting. Dear R. You are being driven from my mind by others.

I wish he was.

I also had a letter from one of my Dublin friends,

Katherine, with whom I have kept in touch. Isn't it odd how one tends to keep in touch with the least likely people. There are people with whom I have been much closer, and yet, we never wrote. But Katherine writes regularly, and I reply. Why wouldn't I come up to Dublin for a day? We could have lunch together. Talk over old times. Really, I would much prefer to discuss intermediate times, or new times, but I said to Jane that I thought I might spend a day in Dublin before the shop opened and my time was no longer my own, and she agreed. So I scribbled a note to Katherine, suggesting a date, and posted it before I could become stifled by lethargy. Sometimes the effort of renewing contact with friends can seem too overwhelming.

Tuesday

Jane asked me this morning if I could drive. It does occur to her occasionally that she hasn't seen me for two years and that I may have done things about which she is unaware.

"I can drive." It is something which Rohan insisted on teaching me. I have a full American licence.

"Can you really? Isn't that marvellous. In that case, you could collect the pottery from what's-his-name."

"Dylan."

"Yes."

She always tries to reduce people whom she either doesn't like or is nervous of by refusing to remember their names. It makes her feel safer.

"And don't let him palm just anything off on you."

"Perhaps you should come, Jane. You're a much better judge."

But she looked flustered.

"No, no. I simply haven't got the time. I'm run off my feet. You'll know perfectly well what to take and what to leave. I'm up to my eyes, as you can see. Don't make difficulties."

What a hypocrite. I don't know why I tease her so

much, because certainly I preferred the idea of going to see Dylan on my own. I suppose I'm always trying to persuade truths from Jane instead of evasions. I would have liked her to admit that she is afraid of Dylan. It would have made her seem so much more approachable. More vulnerable. More like me. She *is* up to her eyes, of course. She has begun to unpack the stock and has set most of it up in the shop, and she is also involved in some last minute negotiations with her bank. I don't know what the negotiations are. I am definitely no longer regarded even as a junior partner. Shop assistant. She did offer me a partnership and I have at least been strong enough to resist that. Anyway, now that I am helping her for the summer, I think she is relieved that I wanted nothing more. This is her own business. She wants no shared responsibility. She wants enough help to debar Berto. No more.

Nick Grant rang me up the other day and asked me to come flying with him next Sunday. I refused and he said that perhaps I would come the following Sunday. I refused and he said that he would ring another time. What persistence. He is so insistent and he has such self-confidence. He cannot even contemplate that I might dislike him. He would think anything other than that. That I am cautious. Teasing. Afraid of flying.

Jane, in a rare egalitarian moment, asked him to her party. I think she surprised herself. It is very funny. I can see her struggling to accept the fact that Berto has gone into partnership with a garage mechanic. Her party has grown with extraordinary rapidity. We had one of those sessions last night when she took out an old Christmas card list and ran through it name by name. She is afraid of giving offence by omitting old but neglected friends in the area.

I suppose she is asking Nick by way of paying a debt

to the fates or whatever. He is, after all, keeping Berto thoroughly occupied. Poor Berto is being worked hard, and is becoming rather resentful about the whole business. Nick has him selling photographs, compiling orders, and the venture is working. Berto sees himself more as an ideas man than as a working man, but Nick is able to manage Berto to his own satisfaction, with Berto doing most of the work and Nick having most of the fun and collecting fifty percent. And the photographs are selling extremely well. I can't believe it, but the ghastly gilt-framed one is the favourite. Of all the ventures one might have wished to fail, this is the one. But it seems that Berto and Nick are doing good trade. Jane says that Berto has a marvellous way with people. He can twist them round his little finger. But I think that Berto himself has been tied into amenable, inextricable knots.

It is quite an agitated house these days. The routine is in disarray, because Jane is rarely at home to organise, and Berto is on the road in his suit, with his photographs. There is still a coolness between them. They are not fighting, nothing so strong as that. But since self is always so firmly at the centre of Berto's life, he cannot conceive that the affairs of others could possibly be of equal interest to his own affairs. And Jane is hurt.

Talk about posing!

There is Dylan now, posing for all he's worth. It must be posing. He couldn't really be like that. So reserved. So enigmatic. So incurious. A cover-up, I'm sure. He's afraid that he may turn out to be a second rate artist instead of the first rate artist he hopes he is. His isolation is all a bit forced. I think he would like to be discovered. And not by Jane.

"Did you never feel the need for a period of

asceticism, Lizzie?" he asked me this afternoon. I arrived up at his house after lunch, feeling thoroughly grousy. It was raining again and there is a leak in Jane's car and water had been trickling down my right leg as I drove along. The thatch had turned grey with the damp and it dripped rain and I walked water into his house on my shoes. There he was, with no fire, sitting in the gloom, reading a book.

"I suppose you'd like coffee," he said reluctantly and when I said, "Yes, please," he had to light the fire. He seems to have so little energy for the mundane comforts. At least he had firelighters.

"Don't drink much coffee myself," he said, and I said, "I suppose you drink holy water," because he made me feel so thoroughly irritated. But you know how it is on a wet summer's day when the wind is from the east and your clothes are damp and you're hoping for a bit of merriment.

"Tea, actually."

But he smiled slightly.

"The rain is shocking," he admitted. "Why don't you sit down?"

He pushed two cats off a chair and they poured like rivers to the floor.

"There."

At least the cushion of the chair was warm from the cats. Once I was sitting, he didn't quite know what to do. I suppose he so rarely has anyone in the house he has lost ease of contact. There are some people who can draw shy individuals out of their shells, make them feel as gregarious as themselves. I am not like that. I simply become uncomfortable and silences extend themselves awkwardly.

"What are you reading?"

It wasn't a book that I had ever heard of, and he

didn't venture any opinion on it, so that attempt died. How do you get to know someone? Surely one doesn't lose the ability entirely? I can't imagine knowing Dylan. How do you get beyond the weather with someone like that? Do you have to wait for a chance connection, some passing judgement about something unimportant which coincides with your own and starts off some deeper level of conversation? How do shy people hop from stage to stage? Abruptly. Blurtingly. I sat, watching Dylan fill the kettle, hang it from the hook, and asked him was he sure he wasn't simply hiding. I think it might have been the sight of him hanging the kettle from the hook. It was all so deliberately difficult. So affected. The loneliness seemed contrived. I mean, the stage setting is so obvious. And then the isolated cottage. The indifferent villagers.

He didn't care for my questions. He is not used to being questioned and he felt that his method of existence was none of my business. He was right of course, but what else could I do but ask questions? There seemed to be no other form of conversation. His small talk is non-existent and I know nothing about him other than that he is a potter and lives alone. That the neighbours and Jane don't like him.

"Why don't you have an exhibition?"

I had stood up again and was examining some of his figures. One of the cats crept up onto the chair I had left. I had this glimpse of a creeping cat, and when I looked around it was flattened in the chair, ears down, chin hanging over the edge. Effacing itself on the cushion.

"Jane thinks your things are really beautiful."

"Do you?"

His eyes were evasive and they wouldn't meet mine. He creates shadows and veils between himself and other people.

"I don't know. I can never judge." I was reluctant to be less than truthful with him. "But that's my defect, not yours. I wish I had some developed feeling for art. I mean, I like them. I think they're lovely. But I don't know whether they're good or bad."

"And your cousin? What gives her that God-like sense of judgement?"

"Jane has that instinct."

He looked unconvinced. "A trading instinct."

He is diffident about his art. You see, he can never be satisfied. When I saw him picking figures down from the shelves, I could see that. He will always be torn with disappointment. Because his birds don't fly. His cats don't stalk. His mice don't palpitate in the hand. His creations can never keep step with his intentions. And because he is so dissatisfied with his work, he is suspicious of people like Jane who come to buy. He can't believe their enthusiasm. He despises the enthusiasm and he thinks it is some flaw in his work which attracts.

He has never had an exhibition. He says he doesn't know how to set about it. Whom to approach. How to select. I think he is afraid of being judged and rejected. He doesn't want to be rejected, because he is doing the only work he can conceive of doing and he can't bear the possibility of being told that his work is mediocre.

"But they are beautiful."

We were choosing ten for Jane and I had the briefest of shivering sensations that yes, they were beautiful. I thought I was being honest, but my own self-distrust in such matters is so prevalent that I blushed when he said, "Oh, you and your cousin. You're both vultures."

Perhaps we are. Filling up the shop with art and calculating profits and overheads and what the public will buy. Bargaining and dealing with art. But Jane says we're doing him a service.

"There's no need to despise us for liking them. Surely our liking your things doesn't change them?"

I was thinking that I shouldn't keep referring to things. But what does one call them? Artefacts? Ornaments? Objects?

"They are what they are," he said cryptically.

It is most disappointing. Really it is. I had hoped he might be someone with whom I could be friends, but I see no possibilities. One cannot deal directly with Dylan. There are too many protective devices between us. He evinces no interest in other people. Later, I was thinking over the afternoon, and I don't believe he asked me one question about myself. And I suppose he'll have me categorised now, the way he categorised Jane, and he'll think he knows me. When I told him I was going to work in Jane's shop for the summer, he just remarked that anyone could be a shop assistant. He could imagine nothing more wasteful of time. Because that is exactly what I have been thinking, I was the more aggravated. I am not afraid of him the way Jane is afraid. But I prefer people to like me, and with him it is impossible to tell. It is difficult to cope with that sort of apathy. I'm beginning to think he enjoys alienating his neighbours.

I asked him did he know he was making himself unpopular with his lobster fishing, and he shrugged.

"There's no law against it."

He has a couple of pots moored out in the bay and every few days he goes out to empty them in his boat.

"Custom is against it. You've probably disrupted complicated rights."

But he wasn't interested. I don't believe he considers his neighbours in relation to himself. He was indeed surprised by the idea that some of his neighbours might not like him. He does no harm and yet he is disliked. He is passive and yet he induces active resentment.

"Doesn't make sense." He kept shaking his head and poking at the smouldering fire with his foot. Because I was so irritated by him, I tried to stir him by explaining how his deliberate asceticism was so tiresome. How it cast a slur on the material aspirations of others.

"Like having a thorn under a nail."

The fire hissed spitefully as a drop of water fell from the bottom of the lukewarm kettle.

"I can scarcely compromise in order to keep my neighbours happy."

He is so precious.

I don't think I have ever come across anyone so self-absorbed. I think he is the closest thing to a small, stony island that I have ever met. He is diminished by it. I think he is suffering from isolation. His face trembles when he speaks to me for all his air of self-containment. I think he is in one of those long, grey depressions which afflict lonely people. And he doesn't recognise his plight. He thinks he is exploring and becoming more self-aware. But really he is receding. He is losing all his warmth and he'll begin to suffer a moral hypothermia.

I realised, talking to him, what it is that has been worrying me about his pottery. It is obsessive. All those animals and birds. Nothing else. He is in retreat from people, and he is trying to give an enhanced importance to clay. Because he has been alone for so long his mind has become extraordinarily fragile. It is likely to crack on contact with others. I think he is in quite a dangerous state of health.

Actually, I find him boring. He is so withdrawn that it is impossible to imagine sitting down with him over a few jars and having a good natter. I thought I might be able to tell him about Berto and the photographs, about Rohan, but I can see now that it would be impossible. He has no curiosity and he seems less human for it. He has made a cult of himself.

I was quite glad when he said he didn't think the kettle was going to boil. I don't believe he wanted me to stay. He could have used the bellows to blow a bit of life into the fire, but he stood with his arms hanging, saying that there was no draw today.

I wonder does he have any girlfriend? Or boyfriend. One wouldn't know his sexual ambience. It is funny how, having spent an hour with him, I think less of his pottery than I did. I can't help seeing it as afflicted. And yet, he asked me to drop by again.

I was thinking about sexual ambience, because, driving home, I passed Jack. He was walking down the main street to the quay with a sheep dog slinking by his legs. Grey jersey, thin, grey, woollen trousers. His face pricked grey by a stubble of beard. Jack was always one to blend in with his surroundings and you could scarcely pick him out from the greyness of the sky and the plastered grey walls of the descending houses. He didn't look up at the passing car and so he didn't see me. He wouldn't have recognised me anyway. I wonder how old Jack is? Berto's age? Older?

I can remember one glorious summer with Jack. I must have been ten or eleven, and he was an enchanter. He had the grey pony and that was an attraction. But the greatest lure was Jack himself. In the summer time he used to give pony rides down on the beach. And I was allowed to walk the pony back and forth on the sand by the leading rein. But it was the other times which were the best. He was never childish. He had more respect. Nor did he condescend. But he knew the needs of a child. He liked to listen to me, which made him unusual enough amongst the adults I knew. And he took me everywhere. He knew the places where the underground rivers seep briefly to the surface. He showed me caves. He knew where badgers had rolled. He taught me how to catch crabs under the rocks with a metal hook. He could recount all the Irish sagas and more besides. I remember he told me that the small, flat oyster shells, luminescent pink, were scales shed from the tails of mermaids, and he didn't expect me to believe him but only to like the thought. I remember riding the pony in the hills, following the sheep tracks, and Jack walking behind.

I never told Rohan. He would have been too cynical. Because the following summer, Jack was banned. There was nothing proven, but it had been rumoured that Jack had a preference for pre-adolescent girls. Poor Jack. There was nothing sexual in his preferences. At the time, of course, I was given no reason for the ban. I was just forbidden his company. I suppose I was oddly unquestioning as a child, but I was used to sudden embargoes. For instance there were things which I did in my father's house which were forbidden in Jane's house. Lighting the fires. Reading at the table. But mostly, I was afraid to question the ban for fear the embargo might have been placed by Jack himself. I suppose I expected him to turn out like all the other adults. To tire of me the way my father seemed to tire.

Later, Jane told me, and I was so angry. I was disgusted that she and Berto should have believed the rumours. I remember how it came up. Jack sold vegetables, and one Friday I offered to go and collect Jane's order. I was fifteen at the time, and when Jane hesitated Berto had looked at me, spotty and lumping out awkwardly from my clothes, and he had laughed.

"Oh, she's safe enough now, Jane. She's far too old for Jack's taste."

I recollect standing there with Jane's wicker vegetable basket in my hand, flushing in that agonising prickly way, as I realised the implications. And that Berto and Jane had thought that I had ... But why could they not have asked me? Why did they rely on the rumours? Jane had said not to be ridiculous. How could they have asked a small child such questions? Perhaps she was right. But it was all so tortuous and deceitful, and I can imagine the agony Jane must have gone through, wondering had anything happened, and should she try to find out, or should she let things rest. And if anything *had* happened, would I be affected afterwards?

I could imagine how the innuendoes had built up around Jack. The fact that he was always to be seen with children. How they used to follow him into the hills. I believe that Jack was one of those people with minimal sexual feeling. He would have felt most at ease with children. He would have sought their company. I don't suppose he remembers me. Nowadays he would be afraid of me. I'm in the other camp now. Did he wonder why I avoided him or did he know? Perhaps there was a deputation. The town is a great place for getting up pressure groups. House-to-house visits. Sign this. Sign that. And they wouldn't have laughed at his protests. They would have waited, narrow-eyed, close-faced, silent. And he would have agreed to cease to be whatever it was that writhed in their imaginations. Certainly, he was forced to take his pony off the beach. No more rides by the moving tide. The rocking, dimpled, horse-drawn sea.

I'm glad I never told Rohan. He would have used the information against me. Recently, when he was demolishing me. He would have accused me of enticement, of deceit and of abandonment. He would have said I had allowed myself to be manipulated by others. He would have called me harmful.

I wonder what the accusations did to Jack. For instance, I wonder if in retrospect he distrusts his memory of the summer he spent with me. I wonder does he reconstruct the summer in the light of what others have said? Do you become what others see in you? A sort of transference. Jane says there was a girl, younger than myself, who claimed to have been molested by Jack. And no one knows was it hysteria on her part, or was it acquiescence in the accusations of others on the part of Jack. They say he has become a recluse. Talks to the dog. Grows his vegetables. Collects the dole.

This evening I was gazing into the kettle as it heated up. The distorted face, the nose spread like cancerous petals. I was tapping idly on the kettle with my fingers, thinking how thin its casing of aluminium sounded and wondering was it getting any thinner. Then I had one of those belly-tightening surges of panic. You begin to decay the moment you are born and eventually your skin is disappearing faster than it is renewing and your bones are becoming more fragile and your blood is slowing up. And I am wasting a whole summer here. I am estivating like a desert lizard. I remember Rohan picking up that childhood name and flicking its tongue at me. A lazy lizard who wants to feed without moving. A lizard who wishes other people to move carefully around her, avoiding casting shadows on her skin.

Jane came into the kitchen while I was tapping and dreaming into the kettle. The door, opening, made the light eddy and flee. A ball of dust tumbled out from the corner behind the door. Mrs. Cleary has become skimpier.

"Don't make it too black, Lizard darling. We like to be able to see the bottom of the cup." Straw tea. When I switched off the kettle the kitchen light began to flicker, and the fridge made a wheezy, droning noise.

"They should put another booster between here and the village. It's disgraceful. It really is. Awfully bad for the motors."

"Why did you come down? You were supposed to be resting while I made tea."

Jane's skin looks thicker than mine. Not thinner. But that may be just illusion.

"I don't want to be old," I said and I felt quite sick at the thought. I only like my body when I don't have to notice it. Even the small pain of a blister disturbs me intensely.

And Jane said it was a mercy how one's contemporaries (she meant Berto) are so tolerant. "They never seem to notice how one ages."

But it isn't the observance of others which worries me. It is my own awareness. The undeniable knowledge of my own decay. The stage where I can no longer run because of palpitations. Looking for cancer spots on the skin. Teeth rotting away. False teeth. Greying hair. Receding gums. I remember Rohan saying during the last week that if we met again in ten years or so, we mightn't even recognise one another. I don't want to lose facet after facet of myself all through my life. And to know that there are important moments which I can no longer remember. And to know that I will die. And to reach a stage where I am always anticipating the event. Sometimes I wish I was a cat or a fish or a bird and had no future knowledge. Which somehow brings me back to Dylan. The way he lives, he's running slow already. As I say, he is losing his warmth.

"Anyway, you're much too young to be worrying about being old. I never heard such nonsense. You should still be thinking that you're indestructible." And Jane laughed. She is lucky. She will go through her life cushioned by prohibitions and approval of others. I do believe that so long as Berto says she isn't old, she will remain as he sees her.

Saturday

The leaves have lost the high gloss of early summer and so have I. And yet there is so much of the summer still to come. It will go churning on for weeks and the days will be repeating themselves. I am limp and ragged and dusty. It is boring to be so confused that even thoughts don't complete themselves. I am full of cramps and spots and lethargy this morning and I can hardly bear my clothes to touch me. I have a period.

There was one maid I remember. She was very young, seventeen. I used to dare myself to enter her bedroom because of a fascinatingly horrible smell. Jane came to stay once, and she discovered the suitcase of used sanitary towels. The girl hadn't known what to do with them. She hadn't believed that blood would burn. At home she used to put them in the river. Maeve, queen of Ireland. Rivers running red with blood of queens. Blood would boil but it wouldn't burn.

Berto was planting trees this morning. A line of twenty pink chestnuts against the fence to the west field. And he actually had a packet of dried blood fertiliser and was tipping a little into each hole and tapping it down with his foot, then sprinkling a handful of earth on top before the insertion of the tree.

"If the Victorians could plant for posterity, then so can I."

He was puffing and dancing ritually round the tiny tree which I held straight for him.

"I thought it was the wrong time for planting trees."

"They're potted. Plant them any time of year from pots. Old stock too. Fellow closing down. Got them dirt cheap."

"They look weakly, Berto."

"Water and blood. That's all they need."

I envy Berto. People like Rohan and Dylan and myself in our generation are no longer fixed into the continuity of things. There are no religious guarantees left. No infinities remain. We all find it impossible to contemplate a mortgage and a pension scheme and the idea of children who might grow up. I think I would find it difficult to plant a tree. It implies such expectations.

Berto stamped on one side of the final tree and it swayed towards him. Then he stamped on the other side and it leaned that way too.

"How can you be so contented, Berto? At a time like this? It is dangerous."

But he either didn't know what I meant or he pretended not to know because he prefers not to be disturbed.

"You're very moody these days, Lizzie," he said, rubbing his hands drily together. "Do you think the hose will stretch this far?"

"No. But it looks like rain."

It was a thundery day. There were clouds, hobbled by the lack of wind, limping tardily, sluttishly, across the sky, barricading a throbbing, angry sun. I had thought of going to beachcomb along the shore, but I was afraid of being out in the open should there be a storm, so I walked listlessly down the drive with nothing in mind. There were some little birds, chaffinches I think, flying before me. Three of them. Even the birds were oppressive today. They were playing with fear. They kept plunging ahead of me down the drive, then waiting and palpitating and plunging again. They made me uncomfortable the way they forced me into the role of hunter and themselves into the position of frightened prey. I ended by flapping my arms at them in the hope that they would fly away.

From one of these trees along the avenue I had a tyre hung by a rope from a branch. I can't remember which tree it was. Swinging from that tyre was the closest I ever came to personal flight. In the heat of summer, the tyre used to leak black rubber onto my clothes, especially across my stomach, because I used to lie through the ring. Then I would fly. There was the cheating, furtive, occasional push with the foot, but for the most part, flight. Rohan once broke his leg flying on cardboard wings from the first floor of his house. His mother found him lying down in the yard, in great pain, but insisting that he had actually flown there. A downward spiral, a gannet plunge. I was more cautious than that as a child. But nowadays I am far worse than cautious. It is as though I have all at once realised how ephemeral I am. A structure in decay. "Lizzie is brooding," Jane keeps saying, and next she will provide a tonic. She puts it down to my broken love affair, and she is probably right. I suppose I was never alone before now. I used to feel indispensable to Rohan, a part of him. However, Jane says this is a passing phase. She believes the pangs of love will disappear, like spots. What I need is to find a nice young man ... I think a nice young man is the last thing I am looking for. It is myself, dear Jane, that I am looking for.

I have decided that I don't want to spend my life being half another person. Bolstering up someone else. Obliterating myself for their needs, and then being turned on for my trouble.

Speaking of flying, Nick is making himself indispensable to Jane. He is almost ingratiating. He brought along a van yesterday to transfer glasses and drink from the Rectory to the Lodge. Jane is beginning to wonder what she ever did without him. Berto is impressed too. Because business is going so well. He can hardly believe he is working so hard. Nick assures him that the hard work is only temporary. He says to wait until it is built up a little more and then they can turn all the trivial work over to someone else and begin to expand. He is egging Berto on, and Berto has become nauseatingly buoyant again. Jane and myself had a row yesterday, because I refused to ride up and down the drive in the van with Nick and she had to go herself. "You'll offend him, Lizzie. He knows perfectly well that it should be you and not me helping him with the glasses. Really, you should be ashamed of yourself."

I wish I *could* offend him. I wish he was so easily repulsed.

"And he's really an awfully pleasant sort of fellow, Lizzie. And he's lonely. He has no family over here. He said to me that he looks on us as a surrogate family." I think I snorted with laughter there and even Jane smirked, though for Jane the reasons differed. "I didn't quite know what to say," she confessed.

As a compromise, I spent yesterday unpacking the remaining stock. You can hardly see Dylan's figures amongst all the other things, and when I see them for sale I can understand how he must feel about parting with them. The shop is so overcrowded that it is impossible to appreciate any one thing. You get no sense of creation. They are just stock, competing for sale in a shop.

When I reached the gateway and it hadn't begun to rain I thought I would walk down to the village and see Mick.

Mick was slicing fat-pearled slices of bacon which fell from the round blade onto a piece of paper held in his hand where they lay, crystallised with salt, pig-backed once again. His second cousin, who helps out in the summer season and who is usually to be found behind the check-out chewing gum and itching listlessly to the radio, was pushing a damp, grey mop round the floor with one hand, making a wisping path up and down the aisles. Out of sight of Mick, she nudged fallen bits of paper in under the shelves with her toe as she faintly blazed her morning trail.

Mick said he thought I must have gone to Dublin when I hadn't been in for so long. And how were things? He'd seen Berto driving through the village several mornings like a bat out of hell. Was he working or what? I nodded.

"And how's life treating you these days?"

I pulled a face and he said he wondered was it that way.

"Too early for an icecream? Or are we watching the figure?" And he looked me up and down. "You'd hardly need to. But still, have a fag instead."

It seemed the most appropriate thing to take, and I pulled one out from the proffered packet. Occasionally Rohan and I would share a joint, and sometimes I like the feeling of smoke in my lungs, to remind me of certain high moments.

"I need cheering up," I told Mick.

"I tell you what. Come over this evening and I'll buy you a drink."

I gave him a look. "Like the last one?"

"Ah no. Not a bit of it. I'll be there tonight. Cross my heart."

"He hasn't got one, love. Never had. All them Gogartys is the same. Born heartless." A woman, waiting for bacon, stood behind me with a basket of shopping. "Are you buying anything or can I go ahead of you?"

"I'll come, Mick," I said. "I'll be there by nine."

"Grand."

Since it was still not raining I decided to chance the beach. It seemed as though it would remain a sullen, dry day. The sun lay, a disc of smoked glass, throbbing a dim but unremitting heat from beneath a film of sulphurous cloud. Below, the sea wallowed yellow and still as stone. I walked out to the neck of the lagoon, and even there the sea was silent, so silent that I could hear the picking noise of water creeping back in with the new tide, unseen, still below the surface of the mud-flats. I climbed up over the grass dune with its mass of close bound flowers, walking reluctantly on the pin-thin leaves of sea-thrift which fold secretively over one another in whorls to hide their centres. The paper pink flowers are paper brown and dead now, the strong smell gone. Sea campion and sea radish rustled and scratched at my legs and then grew silent as I passed, waiting for an activating breeze. There are spring tides at the moment, and at low tide the fish get caught in the lagoon. I could see them, mullet, rising and flopping in the sea. Pools of seawater lay trapped in the fields, shining like watchful eyes.

When I was a child I considered Jane heroic. She was

a soother. She made frightening things acceptable. But now I see that it was that she preferred to be comfortable herself. She and Berto live in an enclosed bubble. A dream. And they are inviting me into their dream. It is too easy. It is too squalidly relaxing. They are the inheritors and they have inherited too much. It has made them slack. They can dream as far as death without ever feeling the pain of waking up. And I could drift along with them, because their dream is so lusciously easy. It is almost acceptable. Almost civilised.

Yesterday, I said to Jane, "Are you ever frightened these days?" And she said, "What of?" Her voice lilted upwards in surprise, her eyes glanced around for tangible bogeymen, and when I said, "Disintegration. You know. The bomb," she brushed impatiently into the air with her hand.

Dismissively.

"We'd be paralysed if we thought of all the things that could strike us down," she said comfortably, and continued to slice fruit for a fruit salad. "Don't even think about it. It's too unbearable. Keep busy." She was peeling the thin, dry ribbons of fibre from a skinned banana and they dropped to the table in curling, flat worms.

"But how can you refrain?"

We joined a nuclear disarmament group in Tucson, but our protests seemed so futile, so puny, so ineffective that I lost my nerve. I tried to stay at home and invent a God for myself. A God that had me and my kind in view. But that was hopeless too. Then Rohan began to tire of me and all the gods collapsed.

"There's nothing we can do about it," said Jane.

It is bad to look into the future too much. It leads to false expectations. Before I came home I was promising myself that this summer I would reappraise, reshape.

But now that the summer is actually here and I drift on as usual, I have begun to think traitorously that next year will be the year. I don't know what I should do next year.

"Stay with us," Jane keeps imploring. "It's so lovely to have you here." And she plies me with food and more food and questions as to my comfort so that I am pampered into ineffectiveness.

The writing? It is impossible to write here. The atmosphere is too soft, too dreamy. Nothing startles here. Nothing shocks. One is too cocooned from events. One is never shaken beyond a faint exclamation of distaste. The other night, they showed dead South Americans, with flies crawling on the faces, on the wounds, and Jane was so angry that she turned off the set. It's not necessary, she kept saying. It was too vehement a picture of violence for Jane. Unacceptable.

In the States I felt helpless. Here I feel even less. I feel disinterested. Removed. In the States we were all caught up in the violent sensation that time could be running out. We were all angry and edgy and watchful. But here, at home, we proceed in a fantasy of games. As though we were untouchable.

Tuesday

The train was a hot, inexorable trap. Too many people. Too much sweat. One of the new trains, the windows were plaques of glass, two sheets to each frame, with a vacuum packed between. There was nothing to be opened. There is such a brownness, such an ill-used feel to a train. The anonymity of the single, brown table leg, the brown veneer top with the scratchings round the edge. Carved initials below the window. Later in the journey, the impersonal mess. Empty cups. Empty sugar packets with the tops torn off. A white plastic spoon with a cold coffee dreg caught in the curve.

Some of Jane's cautions remain. Never sit on a public lavatory seat, darling. So, between Ballinasloe and Athlone, I swayed, cheeks pendulous above the wavering drain, and hoped that all movements would coincide. I remember the embarrassment, as a child, of coming out from the lavatory with sprayed shoes. The uncomfortable belief that everyone knew where I had been and exactly what I had been doing. And Jane asking, in her loud, impeccably articulated voice, "Did you wash your hands, Lizzie?"

And yet, I like a train. I like to sit with my back to

the engine watching the countryside in retreat. The train splitting air to north and south, knifing its line through the midlands. The air tumbling, settling and reclosing behind. The sun doing epileptic flits through the trees. Scenes pass by as unconnected pictures for the eyes. Non-committal impressions. A suffocating copse of trees. A bullock scratching an ear with a back leg, and because he is so quickly out of sight he remains in the mind as a frozen image. To be there forever, perpetually balanced on three legs. The flat fields with squares of trees. The long, electric fences. A ruined Norman tower. The silver towers of a factory, rising like shimmering organ pipes from the apse of a town. A reredos of council houses.

Somewhere beside the rail there was a road, parallel, so wet with sun that it looked like a river. Beside the road, close to the passing train, flew telegraph poles growing green algae. I have always found algae sinister. Too tenacious. I could imagine the algae invading the lines, muffling and sucking up conversations. Lines whining and shuddering. And the algae creating a network of crossed conversations, double meanings, lost intentions. All to be saved by the establishment footholds on the poles. The poles can be climbed, the wires can be treated. The conversations can be recouped. For a price you can even have your conversations improved by a professional cutter. The perfect production, after all, is in the cutting. A season of professionally edited conversations, whereby the cutter divines from the morass of your actual words what it was you really meant to say.

I must have slept on the train.

Back to the echo of the station and the smell of exhaling trains. I bought a fume-polished apple at a kiosk and caught a bus to town.

The meeting with Katherine was unsuccessful. I have a hatred of reunions at the best of times. Those hours spent trying to reconnect. And this time, there was not enough time to make that reconnection. A lunchtime engagement in a crowded pub.

I didn't help, I suppose. I was in a low mood by lunchtime. There had been no traces of Rohan anywhere. Walking through the packed streets, so mobile with people, spending the hour before our meeting, I felt more abandoned than at any time since my return. There are no restaurants where we sat. No familiar shops. No bars or cinemas. There was no particular place where I could stand and momentarily close my eyes to recall our presence. Ours was a city love affair, and any city which bears no traces of him is flat and dour.

The place she chose for us to meet!

Perhaps she was scared. Perhaps she thought that there might be an overspill from the surrounding conviviality of the place should our own conviviality falter. Whatever her reasons, we could hardly hear each other speak. However, with our cheese and onion sandwiches and our beer, we gave each other vivacious accounts of our divided lives since we had last met, and were just teetering on the edge of that void where you either dry up and begin to repeat yourself or you start hesitantly to talk about the personal things which really matter, when she stood up and waved a freckled hand desperately to a man, standing, straining and peering from the doorway.

Gary. Longing to meet you again. Oh, but you must remember Gary. He was a year ahead of us in college.

I didn't recall Gary, and his memory of me had obviously been heavily prompted. He and Katherine share a flat these days. Nothing so definite as an affair, but that is Katherine's way. She won't admit personal facts to any but her closest friends and I am no longer one of those. She was always a reserved girl. Gary bought himself a beer, and prompted by his questions we then repeated large parts of the previous conversation. The more I recollected Katherine, the less likely it seemed that we should maintain friendship. She was always a very precise person. Ambitious. Even in our first year in college she had been both political and vocal, and she had disapproved my defection to the States. She used to mistake my enthusiasm for ideas as determination. She was unaware of my ability to change direction and to lose enthusiasm with stunning abruptness.

She is, I suppose, the sort of person that I, in my most immaculate moments, might wish to be, and that makes her all the more aggravating. She is definite in her goals and dedicated to their pursuit. She is the sort of person to whom it is difficult to come close. If she has cracks, they are effectively sealed. She is also the sort of person who makes one boast in order to cover up one's own inadequacies, so that when she asked me what I was doing now that I was home again, I immediately told her that I was writing a novel, and I managed to make an extremely plausible story about how I was using the experience of helping out in my cousin's business in order to be able to weave it into the scheme of the novel. She was impressed, as she is one to whom writing comes hard. Her talents are for organization. At the moment she is a secretary to an adviser in the Labour party, but she doesn't intend to remain a secretary and I am quite sure she won't.

But back to the fictitious novel.

"You need an agent," she kept saying. "Don't move without an agent." And Gary, who is in real estate and signs contracts to blow his nose, kept nodding in agreement.

"An agent who knows his stuff. Don't touch a contract without legal advice."

Katherine quite unnerved me. She was always self-contained, but now she is self-contained with distinction. She has even developed an elegance in my absence. Silk shirt and a gold chain at the neck. And a hat, a most delightful, undulating summer hat which captured space for itself as she walked it through the bar on her arrival. Her very elegance, combined with some discomfort about the seriousness with which they had approached my fabrication, made me gabble on. I found myself imparting confidence after confidence, and I seemed to grow more gauche and more confused with each sentence and a second glass of beer, while the two of them listened and nodded and even exchanged furtively amused glances. I must say, I thought it most unfair of her to bring an accomplice. They both seemed so composed, so deadly mature, so smug. Oh, they were perfectly nice, and I was pleased to see Katherine and she was even pleased to see me, but I felt at a disadvantage, somehow bare and quite without distinction. A soiled crumpled person from a train. I could tell that I wasn't going to survive their joint post mortem.

We stood on the pavement outside the bar for a little while as we took our leave of one another. There was the final rush of invitations and protestations. You must come to the flat sometime. Next time you're in Dublin, now be sure to call on us. Is that a promise? We smiled falsely at one another and said what fun it had been to catch up on all the gossip, and then I waited for them to move, before turning deliberately in another direction. I was afraid of prolonging the goodbyes further. I am much more frightened by people of my own age these days. They show up my shortcomings far more clearly. And with less kindness.

I called briefly on my father in his office. He dislikes being interrupted at work, but on the other hand, he might have felt hurt if he had heard that I had been in Dublin and had not visited him. Besides, I had evaded one of Jane's ghastly shopping lists, which she produces on the occasion of anyone's departure to Dublin, only by insisting that I wouldn't have time both to see my father and to shop.

He has an office on the first floor of one of the Georgian houses in Merrion Square. A discreet plate on the heavily panelled door announces his name and occupation. He has the drawingroom while his partner occupies the diningroom. The secretary lives in a rather dubious looking slit of a room between the two. A windowless room, lit constantly by electricity and borrowed light which seeps reluctantly through two glass insertions from the other rooms. I believe it was once connected by a lift to the kitchen below, where Messrs. Gambey and Sons now cook contracts and leases and breach of promise. Doubtless it was a cubby hole where the servants concealed buckets of coal, dusters, mops and the evening decanter of sherry.

Miss Chapman, the secretary, has been there for years.

She greeted me with unchanged, faint enthusiasm. How nice to see you again. How well you look. I shall see if your father is free. All in a restrained monotone. I have always felt that she was in collusion with my father to my disadvantage. The organisation is not so much a partnership as a triumvirate, a conspiracy between the three of them. I always saw the linked rooms as a sort of whispering gallery, with all three of them in constant, secretive communication, to the detriment of all clients. They have lunch together each day at a nearby restaurant, and Miss Chapman makes tea and coffee in between, on a kettle whose flex is, and has been as long as I can remember, sealed with red, plastic tape close to the plug. The kettle itself is of old, dull metal, and will work only if the plug is played around with for a short time. More pressure to the left than to the right, so far as I recall. On a couple of unforgettably tedious occasions I was forced to spend the day with Miss Chapman in her office. During crises between housekeepers. So I know many details of her office which would otherwise be secrets. She used to set me visual sums involving paper clips and drawing pins.

"What a pity you didn't let us know you were coming, dear," she said to me before picking up the phone. "We could have made some arrangements. As it is, I don't know ... He's up to his eyes, you know. Still ..."

She has small, blue eyes and an indented chin. All her proportions are small, but her authority is unimpeachable. It would be impossible to by-pass Miss Chapman.

"Richard. So sorry to disturb you, but we have an unexpected visitor. Lizzie. Shall I send her in? Indeed."

It was my own impression that my father had been doing nothing. His desk was quite empty and he was smoking a pipe. I suspect that he takes half an hour after lunch, to smoke a pipe and close his eyes, and that Miss Chapman preserves his time. I am delighted if he does that. It seems eminently sensible. But I don't see why she has to draw a pretence around his activities. And Richard. She used not call him Richard. She enjoys the fact that she knows him better than I do.

I think he was touched that I had bothered to call in to see him.

As a gesture of informality he pulled the client's chair round to his own side of the desk, and we both sat in front of one of the windows, looking out across the street and over the railings to the park.

We commenced one of our usual conversations.

"You're looking well."
"You too. How is Jane?"
"Fine. Sends her love."
"And Berto?"
"Good form."
"Enjoying yourself down there?"

Rather than giving a mere affirmative, I decided that I would enlarge, and I embarked on what I thought was an amusing account of life at the Rectory. The shop. The aerial photography. For once he questioned me closely on my doings with Jane and Berto, and listened with some irritation to the answers.

"You're wasting your time."

I couldn't believe it. He has never before given me such direct criticism. He sat beside me, tilting his chair on the carpet, while his pipe smouldered in the ashtray on his desk and he suggested that I could do worse than to return to college. At his expense.

"In your new maturity," he said, somewhat drily, "you might find it easier to study."

And as he was seeing me off at the front door, he added, "Think about it." And he waved to me as I turned briefly back to smile at him from the pavement. I waved back.

I like the fact that he comes to the door with me. He has a definite scale. With certain favoured clients my father will descend the balustraded stairway and will bid them good day from the front door. As he did with me this afternoon. There are three grades of client. Those that receive a handshake across the desk. Those who are escorted to the head of the stairs and those who merit the most approbative descent to the front door.

On reflection, I am annoyed by his advice. Not by the fact that he has given it to me, but by the fact that he has roused himself from parental lethargy so late. I mean, why did he not give me advice several years ago when I used to long for him to notice my presence? I suppose he didn't consider that I needed advice in those days. I was doing the right things. Passing my exams, intending to go to college.

Funnily enough, Mick gave me almost the same advice the other night. When I went for that drink with him. He was asking me was I not bored? "Look around you, Lizzie," he said when we were sitting at a table while the surly fiddler played. "Where are all the young ones? Gone out of it and you should be gone too. Up to college. Or wherever. This is no place for you." And I remember nodding slowly in agreement.

Dad sees me as turning into another Jane on his demise. Too much money and not enough to do.

Wednesday

Berto asked Jane for a loan and was turned down. A substantial loan presumably. He and Nick have decided that since the photography business is running so successfully, they should expand. No more mere Sunday flights. They wish to purchase a plane. Nick knows of (he would) a second-hand two seater in good shape. Dirt cheap for the condition it's in. The only problem is money. Temporary cash flow difficulties. Slight reluctance on the part of the bank to back yet another of Berto's ventures. The bank wants the company to put up so much of the money before they will consider a loan. And it wants all sorts of sureties. The house. Berto's life insurance. The shop. Jane is baulking both at the idea of lending Berto money and at the idea of relinquishing the shop to the nervous position of guarantor. Jane was an only child, like myself, the daughter of a solicitor. She inherited quite a large sum of money, and the house in Templeogue. She has always guarded a separate bank account, to Berto's chagrin, and she deals with all her own monetary affairs with a certain secrecy. Berto has always been hurt by what he considers to be this strange meanness of hers. He tries to make a joke of it, but I think that underneath he may be seriously offended. In any case, her refusal to lend him money has been a great shock. Up to now she has always proffered loans at his request and now she has refused to lend him money on the one project that he says is really going to make his name.

"You'll have to talk to Jane."

He said that to me this morning, when I came quietly downstairs, thinking that they were both still asleep, and found Berto examining himself in front of the mirror in the hall..He never heard me coming. It was a close examination. The cambered surfaces of his eyes, the mountainous texture of his skin. The hairs which live unenviably at the entrance to his nostrils. All were scrutinised, and the scrutiny was accompanied by sighs. I saw him make horrible grimaces to expose his gums and the stealthy drift of plaque trapped against the hillocks of pink. Berto is not immune from the worry of encroaching age. Those charts at the dentist which show the gums receding, the teeth lengthening and loosening, until the mouth resembles some grotesque incarnation of the horse, have affected Berto. There are other worries too. His hair has receded more on one side than on the other, and this anomaly has created a nervous, brushing gesture with the hands.

I coughed and he jumped but didn't move away from the mirror. Berto says that when he wakes up nowadays, his skin feels crinkled, like an old, stretched garter. Even shaving no longer restores vitality.

"Look at me, Lizzie. Look at me." He was speaking to me indirectly, by way of his reflection in the mirror, and his eyes, from their staring search, watered and shone in the light which was caught by the mirror from the fan light above the front door.

"I'm frightfully afraid that I have passed into middle

age."

And at that moment he looked old. The oddities of light and dark within the house created ageing shadows and pouched the skin to exaggerated crevasses. He is not improved by a slight rotundity. Berto makes periodic gestures towards good health, but is too easily bored by repetition and deprivation. A narrow bicycle wheel of flesh envelops the waist of his trousers.

Jane has given him a blow below the belt. She has withdrawn her confidence in him and in so doing, has caused, if not something as serious as partial collapse, at least a hesitation in his own confidence.

"Without having completed anything of significance."

"Oh Berto, don't be silly."

The trouble was that I couldn't think of anything less inane to say, and there was nothing which I could cite in disproof of his fears. It was then that he told me of Jane's refusal to lend him the money required.

"See if you can persuade her. She listens to you. Really, I think this shop is proving too much for her. Takes up too much of her time and energy. She has become most inconsiderate. Never listens to me any more."

He turned away from the mirror and walked past me to the front door.

"Don't you think she's being unreasonable, Lizzie?" A wheedling tone escaped.

"I expect you've both been working hard, Berto."

"Hmm."

"You haven't shown much interest in her affairs, you know."

"Shunned. You're on her side too. Only to be expected. A pack of women. Thought I'd do a spot of watering before the sun is too hot."

And off he went, to water his dying chestnuts with

their frizzled, dropping leaves.

The trouble is, one doesn't like to witness the rocking of anything which one considers to be permanent.

Jane was in the kitchen, dramatically smoking a cigarette and winding the handle of the mincing machine with her left hand. Congealed worms of raw pig's liver oozed out through the holes. She looked rather miserable. Much as she had looked last night when she had collected me from the station. But last night, when I had asked was there anything wrong, she had said, no, no, not at all, and had rushed into a flight of trivial questions about my day. Whom did I see and what did I do and was the train late, and were the crowds frightful and what did I have to eat? She still tends to treat me as a child to be protected from events, and while she will allow me to show cracks, she cannot allow herself the same privilege for fear of worrying me. Of course, it is also a question of upbringing. The social habit of reticence and pride should be on us at all times, and problems should not be discernible from one's behaviour. Nothing should be allowed to cut too deeply.

Yet even Jane can occasionally be found staring dully at the action of her hands, a cigarette drooping from her mouth. Call it ennui. Call it frailty. A momentary inability to cope with the arrangement of good humour. Don't call it worry.

This morning, however, she faltered. Undermined by the fact that she had heard Berto's voice in the hall, talking with me.

"I suppose Berto has been trying to persuade you to use your influence on me?"

"Well, yes."

"Damn him."

But her mouth trembled and the ash fell from her clenched cigarette. As I have said, Berto is always at his most appealing when he is vulnerable, and now that Jane has wounded him, she most desperately wishes to protect him.

"He's a liability, Lizzie. He really is."

She opened up the mincer and scooped out a mash of raw liver with her finger and shook it into the bowl of worms.

"I've known it for so long really. I can never bear to admit that he's a loser. But who, in their right mind, knowing Berto as well as I do, would lend him money. Oh God, how unkind of me."

She looked at me pleadingly and tilted brandy into the bowl along with a clammy, beaten egg. She stubbed out her cigarette and began to blend her mixture with the electric beater so that she had to raise her voice in order to continue.

"And to offer the shop as surety. Why, it would be sheer madness. It's too bad of him, really it is, to put me on the spot this way." Fragments of egg-coated liver and sausage were beginning to fly and the motor of the electric beater whined and groaned.

"I thought you had confidence in this latest scheme."

"Up to a point, Lizzie. Up to a point. Confidence is relative. Oh damn Berto."

She tipped the paté mixture into a shallow dish and pounded it down with her fist.

"He *would* do this to me just as the shop is about to open."

She hitched open the oven door with her foot and splashed her dish of paté down into a basin of hot water. Then she closed the door. When she turned around, her mind had captured something else.

"Lizzie. Be an angel and do some flower arrangements for the Lodge. I meant to do them myself, but what with one thing and another, I'm behind."

The party is tomorrow night. I looked at Jane in astonishment.

"But Jane! There won't be any room for flowers."

"Nonsense. We must have flowers. Squeeze them in somewhere. A party without flowers! Inconceivable!"

"I think you are perfectly right, Jane."

"What about?"

"The money."

"Oh."

I had brought her back to the original discussion, and the animation receded from her face. She would have preferred me to have said nothing, as she would always rather carry on, get engrossed in events and submerge her worries. She sat down abruptly with a cup of instant coffee she had been making and pushed a second cup over to me.

"I just don't know what to think now. Do you know? Last night I did a dreadful thing. I prayed for guidance. By accident really. I was undressing, and I found myself in silent prayer, so to speak. Frightfully hypocritical to pray about one's capital, don't you think?"

I don't believe she was joking.

The summer is moving with such precision towards disaster.

Cutting sweet pea and roses and some other nameless flowers around the garden, I traced several possible courses their predicament could take, and each of them ended in disaster. In the first course, Jane upholds her principles, refuses a loan, and Berto's photographic business and ego collapse simultaneously. In the second course, Jane lends him the money, the plane is purchased, falls apart, and Berto's business and ego collapse, burying Jane and Jane's shop. There were other combinations which I won't elucidate. I know I should have been able to include courses which led to harmony and success, but they seemed too unlikely.

I am so bored by the confusion they produce and I resent having to be worried by them. It is disillusioning to be adult and to see the flaws in your nearest and dearest. Jane has stage fright. Frequently, when one goes down to the Lodge, there are visitors squinting through the diamond windows, shading their eyes to peer within. But Jane has hardly noticed them. She is paralysed by her temerity at attempting a business venture in the face of all Berto's failures. I think she finds the thought of success almost more daunting than the thought of failure. A sort of flaunting of her prowess in front of poor old Berto. I suppose that there may be a part of her which hopes to fail in order to maintain equanimity, while a large part of her is perfectly well aware of her superior business acumen.

I am bored because I am drawn in just by being here. And yet I am not included. Jane dismissed me this morning by saying that it was nothing for me to worry about. That I wasn't to give them another thought. Things, she said, always work out in the end. Nothing to be concerned about. Nothing more than a passing tiff.

She wished she had said nothing to me.

I am useful to engage as a partisan. But I am supposed to be an innocent partisan. I am not supposed to notice any undercurrents. And even though I might see their relationship much more precisely than they do, I must never describe it to them.

Isn't it odd to have known two people for so long and to be consulted so little? I say very little here. Rohan wouldn't believe my reticence. With him I learnt to attempt truthfulness. States of mind. Jealousies. Fear.

Inhibitions themselves. Nothing was left undiscussed. Perhaps I talked too much.

Last night I dreamt that Rohan had shot off his arm. He was staying in his parents' house, outside Tucson, and I called to see him, unaware. It seemed to be a post-affair occasion. His mother gave me to understand that he was suffering from a cold, but when I went out to the verandah where he was lying in the swinging hammock, he said, "Do you want to see?" and when I said, "See what?" he slipped his jacket off his shoulder and there it was. The shirt sleeve pinned neatly over the stump, like a scene from a movie.

I don't know how he shot it off, and I can't imagine the significance, but I remember asking him where the arm was now, and smiling one of those irrepressible, inappropriate smiles. Rohan would have had fun working on that dream, I'm sure. Perhaps, quite simply, my jealousy is such that I would prefer him blown to pieces than that someone else should have him. How lurid.

I shouldn't be here amongst the chaos of Jane and Berto's complications.

Thursday

You can play the game for a while. Talk about clothes and people and hot baths and oddities of behaviour, but eventually you catch yourself out. A spreading sense of futility. I am not immune to wishing that people should think well of me. I am not like Dylan. But I can't compromise to the extent of changing my mind each time Jane alters her thoughts. It is enough to try and maintain silence.

"You think of no one but yourself, Lizzie," Jane snapped at me this afternoon.

I was hurt by her remark. Considering that I have been seduced by sentimental feelings of loyalty to remain in this bloody place for the entire summer.

"That's not true."

We were both working in the Lodge kitchen, which is small, and even with the window wide open, clingingly hot. We were having an unpleasant time spreading pungent, murky paté on biscuits, spearing pieces of cheese and cucumber onto sticks and trying to avoid stepping on trays of food which littered the floor. It was four-thirty in the afternoon and people were due to arrive at six-thirty. I was eating slices of hot, French bread, spread with some of the paté, and Jane was fussing herself into a crescendo of worry and saying that she didn't think there would be enough food and where the hell was Berto?

Jane was wavering. All afternoon she had been vacillating, and I had been trying to encourage her. But it is odd how people don't really want to be encouraged to do the right thing. They only want to be encouraged to do what they would prefer to do. They like confirmation of their own thoughts, and if they change their minds, they like others to change with them.

As I have said, Jane and I rarely talk on other than mundane things. I know Jane's opinions on most main issues, and I can predict those which I haven't heard. She has heard some of my opinions, and has made them all acceptable to herself by terming those with which she doesn't agree as temporary. But nowadays, we don't discuss those issues on which our opinions differ, because Jane is of the dogmatic school and she doesn't take happily to argument. She is the sort of person who terminates unfavourable arguments by saying, we'll agree to differ, but I think you'll find I'm right, you know.

She opened the conversation herself, as we drove cautiously down the drive with food balanced nervously on the back seat and in the boot.

"Lizzie," she said. "What do you think I should do? Berto is so upset and he keeps looking at me as though I am a viper in his bosom. I can't help thinking I've done the wrong thing."

And, thinking that she was still basically contented with her decision, but feeling isolated, I made all sorts of aggressive, bracing noises and spoke triumphally on her behalf. My encouraging phrases were interspersed with variations on the theme of her first question until finally I became annoyed and said that it was time she put herself first and stood up for her own commitments. Berto, I said, had been spoiled for long enough.

Now, she may have been thinking subversive thoughts like that herself, but the fact that they came from me made them suspect, so that she immediately began to examine her conscience and to compare the advantages of personal satisfaction with the satisfaction of serving the common weal (the common weal, as always, being Berto). The goal of personal satisfaction, in this revised light, began to seem rather selfish.

"He relies on me," she said, and her eyes watered.

"Far too much," I said briskly. I hate when other people start to cry, because I always become weepy with them.

"And I'm letting him down."

There is a limit to the amount of truthfulness one can engage in when talking with relatives. I thought, but I could hardly say, that Berto might eventually be saved from all sorts of discomfort by the existence of one successful business run by his wife. So I merely repeated my thoughts on the necessity for Jane to stand up for herself, which was when she told me that I thought of no one but myself. She was really accusing herself, but nevertheless I was annoyed. I was thinking of something unpleasant to say in return when, fortunately I suppose, Berto arrived with Nick to mix a preserving pan full of some cocktail or other which between them they had invented for the evening.

Berto was looking pale and tight-lipped (somewhat peevish actually) while Nick, who had obviously heard the news, looked sober but understanding. The mediating, third party look.

"Good evening, Jane," he said, with a smile meant to win. "And Lizzie."

But I was an afterthought on this occasion.

"The work, Jane. The immense amount of work." And he spread his arms out to encompass the cramped kitchen, the wilting, smelly biscuits, the trays of sausages ready for the ovens. "And yet you look as fresh as a daisy. There are certain women," he added, lowering his voice, "who simply cannot be defeated by adversity. And I admire them."

There are times when I am astounded by Jane's gullibility.

She may not have altogether believed his compliments, but she liked them. They soothed her and they partially eradicated the effects of Berto's surliness. Berto, meanwhile, had gone staggering into the shop with the preserving pan and was mixing cocktails passionately behind the counter.

Jane said she thought we should return to the house and change so that we would not be caught by early guests. Berto said he didn't feel up to changing. And in any case, it wasn't his party. He wasn't paying for it. The money was coming out of his wife's income. Did Jane mind if he passed round drinks to her friends or would that make him appear too pushing?

"Oh, don't be so bloody, Berto." Jane's voice cracked on the high bloody, and she stormed about the kitchen gathering empty trays about her like shields. "We'll take them with us, Lizzie. Get them out of the way."

Berto stood, an ageing, drooping accusation in the hall as we squeezed past him with our sticky, dirty trays.

"It's the wrong time to make a scene, Berto," Jane hissed at him, gesturing her head towards the shop where Nick had taken over the stirring of the mixture. "We mustn't fight in front of him."

"Fight? Who's fighting? I am merely feeling depressed.

My wife has virtually said that she doesn't trust me."

"I didn't say that, Berto."

"And I'm suffering from a damaged self-respect."

"It simply isn't a good time for me to take on any further financial risks."

"Quite. A financial risk. Your husband."

"Berto. For heaven's sake. It's nothing personal. I'm looking purely in financial terms. Quite separate from us. Do come and change."

Berto allowed himself to be hustled out to the car, and I sat in the back on a seat which was greasy from the bottoms of the paté dishes which had been resting there on the way down to the Lodge.

Rohan should have met my family. I don't think anyone has really majored in psychology until they have met Jane and Berto.

Sitting behind them once again, I was caught by the brief thought that their present estrangement is farcical. This fight is simply another of their schemes. A charade to be played out. Almost a titillation of tragedy in order to experience the pleasure of making up. They both know the parts to take. A tragi-comedy affair, and the length of the tragedy scene is arbitrary and will be stopped short of any real damage. Jane will not remain obdurate. She is already changing her mind. I will be required once again to efface all memory of the difference from my mind.

We negotiated potholes up the drive, Berto steering Jane's car and complaining about the gears and the clutch, Jane sitting beside him, her face averted from his, gazing at passing pot holes which must have appeared filled with tears.

I made my bed before changing for the party. It

occurred to me last night that I might sleep better if the bottom sheet wasn't so wrinkled and the blankets didn't constantly slip in different directions. The feathers in the pillows have been pushed out to either side so that the centres are hollow and the sides are high and hard. There were clothes, clean and dirty, lying about the floor, and Mrs. Cleary no longer comes up to clean the attic. There are limits, she says. I really must sort myself out. I will write some letters too. I shall write to Rohan. I haven't replied to his letter yet. I shall write him a perfectly straightforward letter about the summer and I shall make no pleas. I'll do nothing to put him off writing back to me. I shall write to my father as well, and thank him for his offer. I shall tell him I am keeping it in mind.

I felt incongruous, dressed in the red dress which Jane had bought for me. Somehow taken over. This evening, I didn't feel up to the intentions of my red dress.

I refused a lift down to the Lodge as I was afraid of getting grease on the dress. Besides, I did not wish to be their audience. I might seem hard, but they play at everything they do. They can display myriad surfaces of emotions like the emotions of other people. But underneath I suspect them of being less affected than they seem. Their biggest commitment is towards feeling comfortable. What I dislike about them is that they involve other people and try to mould them as lightly as themselves.

It has been another of those close, hazy days, and the sun, by some kaleidoscopic intervention of dust, had turned a dark red and looked like a festering blister waiting to erupt. I rather wished that I hadn't walked down the drive, as my red shoes proved themselves to be unsuitable and stones and dust kept creeping over the soles and wedging in under my feet. By the time I reached the Lodge there were dirty pads on the leather beneath each of my toes and the skin felt dry and itchy.

I had been dreading the party. Jane and I don't tend to go for the same sort of people. She gravitates towards safe, official types. Doctors, lawyers, well-landed farmers, the occasional TD for colour, colonial relics. And wives of all. Jane feels cowed by women who work and there are few representatives amongst her friends. The occasional secretary, but they hardly count.

I hadn't thought that there would be anybody I knew. I mean, I've met lots of Jane's friends over the years, but I have never managed to know them. Jane's friends are not particularly diverse. There is an underlying similarity which makes them difficult to distinguish. Conversations are predictable and they are all nice in exactly the same way. I was greeted by several of them, and they all said more or less the same sort of enthusiastic thing before peering over my shoulder for someone more compatible. I had thought it might turn into the sort of evening on which one drinks too much from boredom, and one's smile dies *in situ*. However, I was saved from such tedium by the arrival of Tara, who was looking as driftingly, as impossibly, vague as ever. I had quite forgotten that she sometimes lived down here. There is a summer house near the sea to which various members of the family repair from time to time throughout the season. Tara was at Trinity with me and I have always associated her with Dublin and those elongated parties which began when the pubs closed and continued on until lunchtime or so the following day. Weary, deep-probing orgies of conversation. Tara was always fascinated by the subtle gradations of relationships. She could never leave them alone. Her own or those of other people. She had to keep picking and exposing and draining. She used to wear out her friends with her constant analyses. She used to exhaust herself too. But it was her only area of concentration. About everything else she was disorganised and inept. She failed her first year because she forgot to turn up for one of the exams. She was found reading Scott Fitzgerald in a bath mid-afternoon, still unaware of her omission. That was before I knew her. Surprisingly, she had graduated. She has been desultorily weaving throughout the summer. Her sister, who has a loom, subsists (in the holiday cottage) as a weaver and Tara is staying with her for a couple of months because Tom is away. Talking to her again, I could see why it was that one didn't need to keep in touch by something so stilted as letters. Not with one's really close friends. It is with people like Katherine that one communicates. Tara is still with Tom. Tom was the only one of us who had sufficient buoyancy to survive Tara's incessant scrutiny with equanimity.

"He's doing a Ph.D in psychology and he's in the States for the summer. So, I'm waiting and agonising. I'm so jealous. I can't imagine him not taking up with some woman. I mean, it would be abnormal not to, wouldn't it? You see, I told him before he left that he wasn't even to think of me. He was to explore. I told him he could never pick up the American ethos unless he allowed himself to be pulled under, even hurt. And of course, he said that he had no intention of getting involved with anyone. For one thing, he said, he was too content, and for another, he didn't want anything to interfere with his work. So then I really attacked him and said that he couldn't possibly go to America with such concrete ideas. He'd be blocking himself off from experience, and he just laughed at me and said that he was content to have them second-hand in a clinical situation. And now he has gone, and his letters are coming back, full of zest, no mention of women, but a hell of a lot of parties, and I know he's having a rather wicked time and tactfully refraining from saying so and I'm enraged with jealousy, but unable to say anything, since I'm the one who was insisting that he should explore. I can't very well admit that I was only insisting because I never thought he would. Can I? And how are you? Scarred?"

I nodded. "Yes," I said, but I was smiling because listening to Tara had transported me back completely in a way that I had utterly failed to be transported by Katherine. Tara, with her big, shining face and her hair piled messily on top of her head, with wistful, escaping tendrils and several curving combs loosening as she talked and tossed her head. She was so immediately intimate that she transformed the party briefly into one of those Trinity affairs and I began to think for the first time this summer that remaining in Ireland had its possibilities. Tara didn't stay long, as she was on her way to dinner with friends. She had come here in the hope of hearing news of me. She hadn't expected to see me. After the summer, when Tom returns. *If* Tom returns, she added gloomily, or if he doesn't, I must come to stay with them. Or her. If I saw what she meant, which I did. We kissed goodbye and she left, divesting the room immediately of a certain, glowing excitement which Tara carries with her. I feel quite sure that Tom will be back.

The party was actually more successful than most. There was more intimacy than was normal at one of Jane's parties. Jane's idea of a perfect cocktail party is to break up circles which seem intent on getting into serious conversation, and to move people on and to introduce people to other people that they don't want to meet and, in the end, to have that high noise associated with a good party, which in reality is the buzz of people almost shrieking with frustration and inanities.

However, given the shape of the shop, its small size and the clutter of the shelves, it was almost impossible to move. By herculean efforts, Jane managed to force people to circulate for the first hour or so, but by the second hour, she, as well as everybody else, was worn out by the violence of the struggle. I think it would be true to say that they were mostly in static groups by then. Another woman, rather intense, in equally unsuitable shoes, had drawn blood on one of my toes with her heel, and my skin felt no longer dry but damp and tacky where the blood had trickled down to join the dust. At the time it had seemed quite funny and we had clung together, both momentarily off-balanced, falling over the edges of our shoes and giggling. It turned out that she had spent a year in San Francisco, and that it had been the apparent zenith of her life. "And the awful thing is, I didn't realise it was my peak at the time. I took it for granted."

"When was that?"

"The year dot, sweetie. When you were in your cradle. The flower-power years. You know. When we were going to strew the world with flowers and love and we used to send wreaths of withered flowers to generals and presidents and tell them to stay in bed longer, sleep longer, do less damage. It all seemed so simple, so hopeful in those days."

"And what do you do now?"

She was one of those people who crowds one's face with her own and from whom it is difficult to escape.

"I drink," she shouted, for the noise was explosive by then. "I read novels. Nothing political. No newspapers, and when they push the button I'll join the queue for the high dive from the Cliffs of Moher."

Later, I saw her swaying across the Lodge garden and she had discarded her shoes entirely. They were tucked into the pockets of her friend's jacket. She and her friend were singing boisterously and it took them some time to find the gate.

One would never have guessed that Berto and Jane were quarrelling. They are good at public faces. They would never wash their dirty linen in public. Too common.

At the height of the noise when sound seemed to have become solid, and to be expanding and contracting within the room, Jane did one of her impossible introductions. "Lizzie," she shrilled, grabbing my arm and tugging. "You simply must come and meet Bhah-h-h. He is an ex-Bhah-h-h." Her explanations were crushed in sound. An ex-something. What? Ambassador? Minister? Major? Mrs. Someone's ex? It was impossible to know. Quite a stately looking man with tufts of hair on his cheeks. Fired by annoyance and Berto's cocktails. He had seen someone he didn't like. Man over there. Don't know his name. Up at my place six months ago. With plans. Wanted to turn the whole estate over to holiday houses. Said he'd make the house a recreational centre with a restaurant, a sports centre and what he called lounges. And he said he's set aside a top floor flat for us. Asked him why he didn't slap a notice on us calling us an endangered species and charge people a pound to view us through glass-panelled walls. Eating, living and sleeping. Novelty of the eighties. My daughter was quite enthusiastic over the fellow's scheme. She says if we don't let them buy us out, the commies will take over and turn us out. My daughter despises me, you know. Your age. Hasn't got your style at all, what. Pity.

Quite possibly you despise me too. You and she should get together sometime. Wouldn't come tonight. Too nervous. Needs frightful prodding. Stays in her room most of the time. Don't know what she does. Extraordinary. Young people nowadays. Don't you think? Must have a word with that fellow.

Later, when he had drunk many more of Berto's cocktails, he came back, while I was talking to Dylan, and drew me aside. "Don't happen to speak French, do you? No? Shame. Have this French record. Sexiest thing you ever heard. But I can't translate it and my daughter won't. Perverse little ... What? Daresay you wouldn't either, eh? Frightfully prude, your generation." A man quite overtaken by decay. I felt sorry for him. There is nobody left to reassure him that his way of life has been ordained. Afterwards, when I said this to Dylan, he said that was nonsense. I was imputing a guilt to the man which he was most unlikely to have experienced.

I hadn't thought that Dylan would come. He arrived without my knowledge, and I first caught sight of him searching cautiously for his pottery, sliding unobtrusively behind groups of chattering, careless people, glancing over shoulders, under arms, behind heads. We had pushed things as far as was possible to the backs of the shelves, so that they wouldn't be knocked off by straying arms and dropped glasses, and any display that there had been was quite ruined. There were, not unnaturally, empty glasses, half-smoked cigarettes, discarded fragments of food abandoned in the shelves and the stock merely looked in the way. It was amazing how little notice was taken of the shop and its contents. After the obligatory charmings and lovelies, people tended to ignore their surroundings and concentrate on drinking and talking about themselves and each other. I thought that if Dylan did manage to find his pottery, he might be greatly tempted to take everything home with him, so I went over to him, edging my way through those whose glasses were beginning to be filled with increasing generosity by Berto. I had to touch Dylan on the arm before he saw me.

"It's insulting."

"What did you expect?" I shrugged at him and gestured to the simmering crowd. "It's only temporary. Tomorrow, the shop will be elegant again. You should have seen it yesterday. The place looked lovely and I had one of your cats curled up by itself on a windowsill."

There is a pottery cat which sleeps with its nose pressed under its tail. Almost a circle. My favourite cat, and yesterday I gave it a tiny windowsill in diamond-shaped sunshine where it could rest undisturbed. Berto came up, with two empty glasses hanging upside down through his fingers, a jug of drink in his other hand.

I introduced them, but Berto was too engrossed with hospitality to remain in conversation with us. "Have a drink," he insisted to Dylan. "You both look far too serious," and he shook a glass at Dylan. "Lizzie's appallingly moody these days. She needs to be cheered up. Not cast down. This party is for her. To cheer her up. Meet new, happy people. No long-faced people allowed in. So drink up." He handed a glass to Dylan and re-filled mine. Berto leaned towards me. "Jane and Grant are having a heart-to-heart. Fingers crossed, Lizzie."

"Why don't you leave Jane alone?" I asked sharply, and Berto pursed his lips. "Mustn't interfere, Lizzie. Jane doesn't like it. She's not happy at the moment you know." And he drifted away, shaking his head.

Dylan made more of an impression on me this evening. I suppose, by contrast with his surroundings, he appeared as rare. A person with a plan. I don't know what the plan is, but he gives the distinct impression of working to order. A person with some sort of integrity. I was very susceptible this evening. I had been looking forward to his arrival. I hadn't seen him since the day I went to collect the pottery, and since the interval hasn't thrown up much excitement I have been reflecting on Dylan and wondering had I been too dismissive of his withdrawal. With Dylan, there is the sensation that one could be about to break through to friendship and to become close. It is like knowing that there is a very simple answer to something at the back of one's mind if only one could formulate the right question. However, I failed to find the question.

I was dispirited by the way in which people were shifting and caving in all around me and I was depressed by the thought of being tied to the shop for the whole summer through my own fault. I was in a confessional mood, not helped by liberal glasses of Berto's drink.

Up to this evening Dylan had been unapproachable. There is so much coldness to him and his reserve has been too daunting. There is that reserve which people adopt when they are trying to preserve their own quietude, their own precarious peace of mind. I have found him annoying because I have suspected that beneath the reserve he quakes like me. He has hesitancies. He is critical. He is out of alignment. But instead of being drawn to share the likenesses, he has rebuffed me and has preferred to keep distance between us.

I think it was the sight of him descending to the frail humanity of searching for his own clay animals on the crowded shelves in the middle of a party, and actually demonstrating petty disappointment, which made me say, after the departure of Berto, that he was so difficult to talk to and yet he was the only possibility.

"Thanks," he said, which could have meant anything, but in my mood of desperation I took it as an invitation to speak freely. First of all, I told him that I found it very disheartening to expose bits of myself and to be given no confidence in return. I didn't mean, I said, that I wanted him to break down and confess his shortcomings and the hardness of his life. But it would be nice if he could occasionally admit doubts.

"I admit doubts. Better now?" His enigmatic smile remained, but at least he was looking at me and not over my shoulder. I was scarcely deflected by his comment, which in passing annoyed me by its condescension. I become garrulous at parties.

"No. Not in the least bit better. Look at your smile. It gives nothing away. I mean, one can't talk to an effigy. You have said you have doubts, but that is meaningless. It seems to me that you won't come down and examine actual people. You take this lofty, meaningless position of isolation. I think you are so busy preserving your own integrity that you won't allow yourself to know people like me from the enemy camp for fear of being undermined into a sneaking liking for them."

And then, to my mortification, I burst into tears. Talk about the self-pity of the drunk. I didn't actually feel drunk. I just felt overwhelmingly sad. I had forgotten that tendency of mine to cry when drunk. Anyhow, there I was, sobbing quite loudly (not that anyone other than Dylan noticed) searching uselessly for a tissue, when Dylan put his hand on my shoulder and said, "It's too hot. Let's go outside to the garden." So off we went, pressing through the masses with me snuffling unpleasantly into my hand, and Dylan holding my other hand, and shrugging his shoulders this way and that to make a passage for us to the door. The party had overflowed, and there were guests, inebriated and sober, arrayed on the lawn.

"Let's walk a little way up the drive," he suggested.

Under the trees which were stiff in the windless evening I pulled up a bunch of long grass and did what I could for my nose.

"Sorry," I said, and then, because my toe was so painful, I put an arm through his and hobbled beside him on the grass.

The night was still warm, though the weather was changing. The dim, haze-hidden stars were being stalked and captured by a black mass of cloud which had been collecting on the horizon throughout the afternoon and which was now rising slowly up the sky. I have been so busy considering how I see Dylan that it never occurred to me until this evening to ask how he saw himself. Not that he answered directly. He has no intention of subjecting his own peace of mind to my scrutiny. He doesn't wish to be disturbed. But there were things he said which I found disconcerting. Half-way up the drive he asked was I cooler now, and did I feel calmer. My toe had begun to bleed again. I could feel the wetness of the blood slipping on the insole of my shoe.

"Perhaps we could sit down?"

"Your dress. Will it not be ruined in the grass?"

I took my hand out from where it linked through his arm and I crouched down to thread my fingers into the base of the grass.

"Dry as a bone," I said. I sat down and pulled off my shoe. The relief of taking the weight off my foot set my toe throbbing with pain. Dylan sat down beside me and sighed lightly.

"I'm tired," he said. "I was fishing late last night."

"I didn't think you would come this evening," I said.

"I wanted to see you."

"Oh."

He said it so indifferently I was hardly flattered.

"You seem different to your cousin."

"You misunderstand Jane." It seemed important that he should know about Jane and I gazed at him. "She's harmless. She's even well-intentioned." Tears collected in my eyes again, as I thought, sentimentally, about Jane. But he shook his head impatiently. He had drunk very little.

"They're all tainted with the same shallowness."

I didn't like the way he dismissed her as a class. Maintaining his purity by an unseeing hostility. I feel uncomfortable when someone belittles my relatives. It is one thing for me to be critical. It is quite another for an outsider to judge.

"She wants to patronise and display," he remarked and he lay back, his arms making an irregular cushion behind his head.

"She's kind."

"It's easier to be kind," he sait bitingly. "You're a fool if you think that kindness is necessarily a virtue."

It is disconcerting when someone detached pinpoints your own misgivings. I felt judged. I myself have thought that I have been undermined by Jane's kindness this summer. His observations didn't incline me to like Dylan any the better.

"I am very fond of Jane," I said coldly and I sat up straight.

"Don't take offence at the truth," he said. "You wanted to talk. You've just committed the very personal indiscretion of weeping at me. You can hardly withdraw now. What do you want to know about me? What lack of intimacy makes you cry?"

I eased back on my elbows and looked at him. I was

wondering how old he was. Not that much older than myself. Too self-contained. In dull moonlight, his face was inscrutable. The trouble with Dylan is that one won't break through the barriers. He is so goddamned serious. He induces in me a debasing sense of levity. The wish to tickle him in the ribs, flick him under the chin, trip him up. Somehow break his composure. Lying back on the grass, asking me pompous questions. I suppose I didn't care for the criticism which was creeping into the conversation. I had been looking for sympathy.

"Oh, forget it," I snapped. "I was crying for the fun of it. To make a scene. Because I have to work for the rest of the summer and because my love affair is broken. Don't you remember? Jane told you. Not that she spelt it out of course. She's too polite for that."

"You're in a dangerous position, aren't you?" he asked quietly and he drew a circle on my shoulder with a dry piece of grass. "You have good intentions but you allow yourself to be manipulated."

It is not a thing one likes to be told.

"I owe Jane a summer."

"Cousin Jane? And after the summer? What then? She won't notice your sacrifices. She'll only notice the discrepancies. She'll take all your compromises, all your trumped-up sense of duty for granted, until you begin to accept them yourself and you'll end up just like her for want of something better."

"You're presuming a lot."

"Oh yes. I'm presuming that your Jane is like my mother and my sisters. They are time wasters. They fabricate dreams and motives and they draw everyone into the fabrication."

"And do you feel no obligations?"

"None."

"They think they know what I should be doing." I

must have sounded childishly complaining and he yawned, closing his eyes and opening them again, blinking tears of sleep away.

"What do you want to do, Lizzie?"

A disconcerting question. I stood up abruptly and shook my dress free of broken grass. I slipped my shoe reluctantly over my foot and began to limp back down the drive. A chilling question.

"I don't know," I said very quickly over my shoulder. He caught up with me and slipped an arm round my waist.

"Lean on me. You're closed in, aren't you, Lizzie? Trapped."

"What should I do?"

It seemed such an easy question to ask while leaning on someone's shoulder, when the moon had disappeared behind a cloud and you are all alone in the dark. But he laughed.

"How should I know?" Even the grass at the edge of the drive was painful to walk on in the dark because of unexpected stones scattered from the avenue by the daily passing up and down of cars, and a couple of times I drew my breath in with pain on knocking my toe. He didn't seem to notice and we continued unevenly and jerkingly down the drive towards the Lodge.

"You think you've found yet another person who'll tell you what to do," he remarked suddenly and rather abrasively. "Someone else who'll save you the responsibility of thinking for yourself. You feel at liberty both to despise me and to pick my brains."

Yes, I do despise him. He refused me any help. He's so busy preserving himself, his soul of polished integrity, that he can't afford to be generous.

"You're selfish."

"No I'm not. You're not allowing yourself to grow

up. You want to live off other people's morality. Instead of working out your own. I wanted to see you again because, as I say, I thought you might be different."

"And?"

I could feel him shrug.

I thought I was more like him, but he apparently doesn't think so. He does not hold me in very high regard. Which is galling. I find that I begin to like him more as he begins to like me less.

By the time we reached the gate leading into the Lodge garden, warm drops of rain had started to fall. There were the last guests running hastily to their cars while Dylan stood beside me with an arm still round my waist, waiting for them to leave. "You'll get wet, walking home." I said. I could see his face again because there were headlights shining, dissecting us and carving us with light as the cars backed and reversed and turned. He is a slight man. I am tall but he is barely taller. He has a darting, evasive dimple which appears on his left cheek when he smiles. Which I like. I considered whether or not we might attempt a goodnight kiss on the grounds that I had wept at him and bled at him. But the thought of kissing him seemed a bit incongruous, and he might indeed have refused, which would have been embarrassing, so I disengaged myself from his arm and thanked him and said goodnight. I thought, as I was walking up the short, flagged path to the Lodge, that I might have offered to drive him home in Jane's car, but then again, why risk a refusal. Besides, my toe was sore and I was tired.

"Oh, your poor toe," Jane said when she saw it. "I think you're going to lose the nail. It's gone black. They say you should pierce a hole in it, to let the blood escape."

"Sounds like a way of giving yourself tetanus," I said. I felt quite sick at the thought of anybody touching my throbbing nail. "It's raining. Has everybody gone home?"

"Yes."

"Even Grant?"

"Yes. Have a sausage."

She and Berto were sitting in the kitchen, eating cold sausages and plain French bread. Jane looked faded with tiredness, and her hand, as she lifted a piece of bread up to her mouth, shook. But Berto's cheeks were high pink and he was holding Jane's other hand in his own.

"Well?" I said interrogatively.

"Wasn't it a lovely party?" asked Jane in a rush. "Masses of food and no one became objectionable. Did you enjoy yourself? I saw you talking to Dylan for a while. What did you find to say to him? You *are* good."

She wasn't going to tell me anything. I had interrupted them and they wanted to be alone but couldn't bring themselves to say so.

"Could I take your car and drive back to the house, Jane? My toe is so sore. You can come with Berto. Unless you want to start washing up tonight?"

"Oh no. We have the whole day tomorrow. You take the car. Have a nice hot bath when you get back to the house."

"Goodnight then."

"Goodnight."

"Goodnight."

As a child I was frightened of the dark, and I still have remnants of that fear. There were no lights left on in the house and once I had closed the front door behind me and had walked from the outer hall to the inner hall, I was stalked by uncommon shadows which set my back on edge. I hate a place to be so silent that you can hear yourself swallow. I ran very quickly up the stairs to the attic and turned on a transistor to hear some evening music.

When I was a child and I slept alone, I used to sing to distort the silence, but I was never wholly successful in allaying fears. There were heavy, black-lined curtains across my window which muffled sound. They also caused incoming light to break up and separate into segments of light which ran like living things on the walls and ceiling. It made the nights somehow worse to see those fragments from the lights of passing cars reflected in the room. The safety of the room was only relative, tenuous, when the night could not wholly be obliterated. There was the feeling that night was an animal crouched outside, growling softly, many-eyed, only barely held at bay by the glass and the double-layered curtain. I would never open a window even on the most suffocating of summer nights. The closed window was my frail protection. Opened, the animal night might ooze in and I would be quite enclosed. The inside noises did not counteract my fear. They did little to reassure because they were always startling. Sounds from downstairs were minimal. Certainly there was sometimes the sound of the radio, either from the kitchen where the housekeeper would sit, or from the drawing room where my father sat. From both places indeed. But human noise was rare, and when it came, it only served to frighten further by its unexpectedness. A cough. The opening or the closing of a door. Or more uncannily still, a sound of laughter, maybe in response to the radio.

I had no protective devices then. The memory of my

mother was the obvious source of protection, but it was one which I couldn't use, because I didn't trust my memory. I thought I could recall my mother, but I wasn't quite sure. It was a great anxiety to me, this lack of certainty. That the recollection should be no more than tentative meant that I could never concentrate on the memory as a talisman. For fear that I might be recalling, not my mother, but some other woman. Were I to pay full homage to this doubtful memory and should it turn out to be false, I could envisage great anger emanating from the soul of my real mother. It would be akin to worshipping a graven image. To me, the word graven was inextricably linked to a woman, not my mother, rising from a suspect grave as a snare for gullible children.

But tonight it was surely too wet for ghosts.

I brought the radio along to the bathroom with me and turned it up loudly while water from the taps thundered into the bath and steam swallowed up the edges of the room. The bath stands on lion's claws and the lip curls like a petrified wave. There is satisfaction to be gained from lying in a very hot bath while rain plunges against the windows and gobbles in empty drains.

I should never have come here.

I should never have left the United States.

It is so easy to re-plan the past. But at the time I was too confused by Rohan to make my own decisions. I suppose one spends one's life having one's decisions confused by the influence of other people.

I am frightened by change. It is a deficiency, I know, but I become stupid with fear. I remember the fear I felt on the first day I knew that Rohan had grown tired of me. On reflection, there had been times before that day when I simply hadn't understood the meaning of things he had said. He had said things which, in retrospect, I could interpret as cruel, but which at the time hadn't hurt at all, because I had interpreted them in a different light. But that day, during December, was the one which speared me with the first pain of rejection.

We had a third floor apartment, Spanish style, open-plan with archways, square and curved, dividing areas of space. The whole apartment block was custom-built. There were about forty apartments, fully furnished, in blue or green or gold. Ours was gold. They were spacious places, a bit false maybe, but pleasant, unobjectionable. Anyway, this evening a friend of Rohan's called by. He'd been out in California and was back visiting. He wasn't a person I knew and I can't even remember his name. We were drinking cans of beer and he was wandering around the apartment, talking cautiously, the way one does with friends whom one hasn't seen in a while. He was saying innocuous things and admiring the apartment. "It's so big," he was saying. "I hadn't expected such gloss, Rohan." And Rohan had lifted his hands. "I was sort of jumped into it," he said. "When Lizzie goes home, I'll rattle around in this place. Guess I'll have to sell it and move somewhere smaller." I laughed and said, "But I won't leave you, Rohan," and he looked at me and said "I'm quite afraid you won't."

I remember sitting there for another five minutes or so, without speaking while Rohan and his friend talked. Then I stood up, said I had to go out somewhere and would they excuse me. I remember Rohan watching my face as I spoke. I walked around Tucson for hours feeling churned up with panic, trying to convince myself that he couldn't have spoken the way he did. That I had misheard his inflections, that he had been practising a black joke. It was then that my memory forced me to recall other incidents. The way he had called me his appendage, and I had thought he was teasing me and I had laughed. And had disregarded the fact that he hadn't laughed with me. Other things.

Later, as his disenchantment grew and his impatience with my refusal to understand escalated, he became far blunter. The telephone calls, the absences, the boredom, the fights. Once he even suggested that I might like to take myself off to the pictures while he entertained a woman he knew well. He apologised for that.

But that day in December was the worst day.

I am ashamed of how long it took me to leave. To be dislodged. I wish now that I could have left with dignity. Now that I am safely home. But when I was involved, I was too stunned. I descended to pretence. To blindness. To a deliberate rejection of the facts. Instead of planning a sensible withdrawal, I spent all my energies convincing myself that Rohan's rejection was only temporary and trying to regain his love. It makes me squirm to think of my strategies, but I loved him still. When I think of how I used to weigh and balance the smallest, unreflecting acts of kindness which Rohan displayed in those last months. All the things I took to be turning points, indications of revival. He must have been disgusted by me. There was a cactus which grew out there, a chain cholla, it was called. When one brushed against a plant links of the chain would snap off, attaching themselves painfully to whichever parts of the body they happened to touch. They were very difficult to detach. I was the same. Once he went away for a week, without telling me in advance. He left a note and some money in the kitchen. The note didn't say when he would be back. I should have left the apartment in that week, but instead, I waited, mesmerised, scarcely eating or sleeping, to see would he return. When he came home, he accused me of not wanting to grow up. Like Dylan accused me tonight.

I was roused from self-examination by the sounds of Jane and Berto coming in. The bang of the front door and their voices as they climbed the stairs. The bath-water had grown cool and scummed with soap. They closed their bedroom door and I got out of the bath, dried myself and went to bed.

It is awful how something so small as a toe can keep you awake for most of a night.

When I came downstairs this morning, Jane was being brisk and uncommunicative. She was wearing slacks which don't suit her at all because her bottom is too big, and she wouldn't meet my eyes long enough for me to question her about last night. She wouldn't stay still.

Berto had already left the house, to sell yet more photographs. Now that he has covered the immediate area he is having to work even harder to retain the original sales momentum. He says he can see why commercial salesmen top the charts for heart attacks and nervous breakdowns. There is a terrible temptation to better last week's sales. He is also discovering that people work during the day. And they don't always make up their minds at once, no matter how hard he pushes them. He sometimes has to make two, even three visits before a sale is made, and sometimes it isn't. His weekends have gone. Usually he is a bit lethargic by Friday, but today he had flown like a bird from the house. Propelled by what?

Jane didn't tell me until we were once again enclosed in the kitchen, clearing up the mess from the party.

"I know you'll think I'm mad," she said. I went on drying the glass in my hand.

"But I had to help."

"I suppose Grant persuaded you?"

"No, actually. Berto did. His face you know. I couldn't bear it. I wish I hadn't ... the lack of faith. I let him down."

I made one of those dismissive sounds as I packed the dried glass into one of the cardboard boxes in which they would travel back to the house. She looked at me.

"You're still too clear cut, Lizzie. You wouldn't understand. You don't know how interwoven the layers of trust are."

"I said nothing, Jane. It isn't really any of my business."

Layers of complicity more like. She wanted me to tell her that I approved. To shift with her, and I couldn't do that. We worked on in silence. She must have been wishing that she could talk to Berto and not to me. Now that they are in difficulties, she would rather I wasn't here, watching. She would have preferred to be alone, talking to herself and reassuring herself with the right replies than to have me there, listening and disapproving, however silently. She made me think how awful it must be to have children growing up and watching your decaying relationship. Not that their relationship is in decay. Their principles are in decay.

"It wasn't worth disturbing the peace. We've been so content up to now. It would have been cruel to upset it."

"I wish you'd told me nothing."

"Oh Lizard darling. You are selfish."

I suppose I am. Sometimes I think that the only way to remain intact is to keep your thoughts to yourself. And why should I be disappointed when Jane acts exactly the way I imagined she would act? What right have I to expect her to change? She looked so worried bending over the sinkful of water, chasing glasses with a sponge. I leaned over and kissed her on the cheek. She smiled faintly.

"I'm sorry," I said. "I'm sure Berto is a revived man this morning."

By afternoon the shop was tidy again and we were ready to open the following day. Jane thought she might rest for a couple of hours. "Goodness knows when I'll get the chance again."

I decided to go for a walk. As I was leaving, Jane called out to me, "Why don't you drop in on Dylan? I was so glad to see you making friends with him last night. You're too solitary, Lizzie. It's not good to be alone so much at your age."

"I'm happy."

"You should have lots of friends. I had lots of friends when I was your age."

"Bye."

And now you have Berto, Jane darling. Aren't you lucky. You and Berto, crushing one another to death.

It was a damp afternoon. A changeling wind. Light, misty rain blew in spasms. Veils of rain drifted moodily, feather-edged, over the hump-backed hills, and the valleys between looked steeped in trapped, warm rain. The scent of the earth and of the flowers by the roadside was lured out with drops of floating rain.

I walked down to the quay and found Dylan standing in his boat, baling water out from under the boards.

"How's the toe?"

"Pain gone. Are you going fishing?"

"Just as far as the neck. The tide's too low to go any

further."

"Could I come? Jane says I'm too solitary."

"Please yourself."

"You're so welcoming," I said, as I crept down the steps to the boat. The lower steps were slimed with green weed. Dylan leaned over and took my hand. I admire people who can stand easily in a boat. I climbed cautiously in and asked where I should sit.

Half-way across the lagoon he told me that he wasn't fishing. He had come out to make sketches of the terns fishing in the gully, where the tide was still rushing out.

"You'll have to be perfectly quiet," he warned me. "We can get in very close to the gully with the boat if we don't make a sound."

He continued to row towards the screaming cluster of terns and the boat thumped on the water at the edge of the current. We were approaching the gully from the side, and even out of the main pull of the receding tide the boat moved fast. The mudflats were emerging from the dropping sea, and oyster catchers and curlews were flying down from the nearby rocks to probe the soft muck for food. I used to dig up lugworms there. Carving out the mud around the airhole with my plastic spade. The chunk of mud splitting and collapsing from the spade. The grey worm. Like a vast maggot. I used to fish with a lugworm pierced on a hook.

"I'll take the oars if you like," I offered and he nodded.

"Right."

We changed places and the boat tilted back and forth like a see-saw. Dylan settled himself down in the stern of the boat and took out a sketching pad. The prow of the boat had risen high out of the water, so I moved the rowlocks up to the next set of holes and changed to a seat nearer the front.

"There'll be quite a pull when we get nearer to the channel," he warned. "You'll have to lean hard on the oars to keep her still."

I rowed down parallel with the mudflats.

"I want to be a writer."

"What?"

"Last night you asked me what I wanted to do. I want to be a writer."

"How many hours do you spend writing each day?"

"I don't have the time."

"Oh Christ."

"Sometimes I start something and it peters out after a page or so. Ideas. They seem so exciting until I write them down."

He looked over my shoulder.

"Close enough," he whispered, and I leaned on the oars so that water gushed past the braking boat. The boat was out of the main rush of the tide, but even there she bucked so that I had to keep constantly dabbling and stabbing with the oars to hold our position.

We stayed there about an hour and it was chilly and boring. I couldn't even glimpse Dylan's sketches, because he had his knees bent up as a makeshift easel and the pad was hidden. I could hear the terns and the constant splash of their diving and the churning of the tide in the gully, but it took an effort to turn my head around to watch them and every time I tried to manoeuvre the boat to a different angle, the force of the water pushed it back and it was all I could do to hold her still. The misting rain which had been hanging in the hills grew heavier and began to roll in over the bay.

"Rain coming," I said.

"Damn."

He looked behind him. Only the line of the dip between the two closest hills was still visible. The high lines had disappeared, though there was still the bare sense of shape for the mist hung darker where it was backed by the hills. He shut his sketch pad and put it in a plastic bag with the sticks of charcoal. The rain grew heavy as I was rowing back beside the mudflats and the pier at the foot of the village grew faint.

We were soaked by the time we reached the harbour wall, with water running down our faces. I could feel rain collecting inside my jeans while I was still rowing, and when I stood up to climb out to the steps, a small stream of water ran from my thigh down to my ankle. I squeezed my hair out on the pier, waiting for Dylan to come up the steps.

"Let's go and have a drink," I suggested. He hesitated, and I said, "Oh come on. It'll warm you up."

We ran up the hill as far as Donovans with the rain pelting down and the rising wind blowing against us.

Donovans was quite full and the floor was damp with footmarks. We bought ourselves a couple of beers and went over to a free table by the unlit stove. I hate the sight of an unlit stove when I'm cold. It accentuates the misery.

"Do you ever come in here?"

"Occasionally."

He makes me nervous with his protracted silences, and, as usual, I talked too much. He has that effect. I feel the need to fill in the silences. Which I did by most disloyally telling him of Jane and Berto's differences of the past few days. "And now she has given in. She's lending the money to Berto."

"So."

"Well, I think it's awful. Don't you?"

"Oh, not particularly. Why should I?"

Why do I have to say too much? There I was, having betrayed Jane's confidence and Dylan was obviously bored. He had no comments to make and he was drinking fast. I supposed that I must have wasted his afternoon, or at least that I must have disturbed it. The trouble is, I enjoy talking to people, and last night I really thought that Dylan had become friendlier.

"Why do you retreat when we might just become friends?"

He looked at me and drained his glass. He stood up.

"I'll buy you another," he said and walked off to the bar.

When he came back with the two glasses, he put them down on the table and pulled his chair closer to mine. He sat down and leaned his arm tentatively on the back of my chair.

"You see, Lizzie," he said with that slight smile of his, "I think you might be merely using me."

"What do you mean?"

But he dismissed the question with a flaunting hand.

"You're making yourself comfortable for the summer, and I do believe that if there was one more congenial person around, you wouldn't be here with me."

"Maybe that's true. I don't know. But isn't that the way things start? By convenient proximity?"

My face had reddened. He laughed and leaned a little closer to me. "Oh come on now, Lizzie. Be honest. You don't intend to start anything. I know what you think about me. You think I'm odd. Inadequate perhaps, but less inadequate than the others. So you'll come and you'll waste my summer. You'll force me to like you. And then you'll leave, refreshed, at the end of the summer. Having recovered direction. And afterwards you won't give me another thought. You won't even remember me."

He had put his hand on my shoulder and I could feel it tensed, the fingers tight on my shoulder blade. "I'm only significant to you now because of the very traits that will let you forget me later on."

"Oh Dylan, don't say that," and I flushed deeply because I thought that he might have spoken the truth and it sounded so callous put that way.

"Not that you give me much to remember you by," I added defensively. "I know nothing about you. I have been talking away about myself and you say nothing."

"What is the point in opening myself out to someone who is merely looking for summer entertainment and who will then forget me?"

"Nothing venture, nothing gain," I said lightly and I made a small face. But I felt guilty. He was right. I didn't intend to start anything. I was only looking for someone with whom I could while away the summer. Someone to talk to. I would not be staying on in the autumn. Why should he offer himself up to my whims if that was how he saw my advances? There was nothing to say he should, apart from the tradition of normal, human friendship.

"My ventures always end up in loss," he said gloomily and he withdrew his hand from my shoulder. I looked at him with my eyebrows raised, thinking that perhaps he was about to divulge something, but he stood up again. "See you around," he said and he went out to the street.

Poor Dylan. He would much prefer to dislike me.

I stood up quickly and ran out after him. The rain had stopped and the cloud was beginning to break. He was standing on the pavement, pulling his sodden jersey over his head, the bag with the sketch book held between his legs.

"Why are you living here, Dylan?"

His head emerged, hair ruffled, face pink.

"I told you, Lizzie. It's a phase. An aesthetic phase. A need for peace. A need to recoup my losses. And now that I have told you, what are you going to do with the knowledge? Nothing that will be any good to me."

"Does that matter?"

"Oh yes. Greatly. You mightn't understand. People like you, with your big egos. Well developed to survive."

"I'm sorry," I said and I turned away.

It must be terrible to have qualified friendship so much that he has put it beyond his reach. He believes in nothing. Not even in himself. He is more helpless than anyone I know. Sliding ineffectually on his own frozen cynicism. I remember the disillusion of playing with ice myself. The burning, searing cold of my hands. The pain of my fingers. How they lost their ability to mould and shape. Until today I thought his attitude brave, but now I see it stems from fear. I was thinking of Tara and Tom as I was walking home, and how Tara urged Tom to let himself go. Really she was only advising him to continue living. Dylan was trying to turn an offered friendship into something cruel, something calculated.

Thursday

Something happened in the shop today which made me want to leave. I have always felt an outsider in Ireland. A voyeur, peering at the real life of Ireland. Catholicism. Nationalism. And all the celebrated Irish characteristics. But I am Irish enough to feel intense rage at efforts to exclude me. A woman came into the shop this morning. From Cork, by her accent. She was looking for a gift to send to a relative in America, so I had to spend quite some time helping her to make a choice as she was worried about weight and bulk and breakability. When we finally decided on a crocheted shawl and I was wrapping it up, she suddenly began to attack my accent. It was a shame, she said, to have girls like me, with our jumped-up accents, serving Irish goods in what was supposed to be an Irish shop. And where was I from anyway? England? Weren't there plenty of Irish girls looking for jobs without filling the vacancies with the likes of me. I told her coldly that I was Irish and continued to wrap the shawl, folding it into tissue paper. And then she had the nerve to pat me on the hand and look knowingly at me. You'd be better off so, she said, dropping the accent. I started to explain, and then I stopped. What was the point? In fact, I couldn't explain, because my chest had tightened and my legs were shaking. I felt cornered by her, squeezed out. Jane couldn't see why the episode had upset me. She thought it was quite funny. You should have spoken to her in Irish. That would have foxed her. But I didn't want to do that. I wanted to be allowed to be myself. It was the monomaniacal idea that there is only one possible type of Irish person which frightened me.

We have had a lot of visitors to the shop. Tourists like glazed cherries from the unaccustomed Irish sun. Jane is thrilled. She has been keeping a tally on numbers and Berto is impressed with the figures. He is becoming involved, despite himself, because he rather likes the shop. He has come in several times and has lingered for an hour or so, reluctant to leave. He enjoys customers. He chats with them about politics and the economy, and sells a surprising amount as he talks. He says that the change from the door to door drive is an undeniable relief. And he feels in a different position of course, with the customers being on his territory rather than the other way round. The initial impetus is not his.

And Jane brightens up when Berto comes into the shop. He is so much more enthusiastic than I am. She doesn't understand how I could be bored. "But it's such fun, Lizzie. We're on the go all the time. There isn't a minute to be bored. No time to brood. Just what you need to take you out of yourself." Berto, on the other hand, loves charades. He loves parties, and to him, the shop, with its customers coming and going, is a sort of eternally extended cocktail party. Endless snippets of conversation. The opportunity to be charming and the feeling of extending hospitality. I don't think anything he has ever done has suited him so well as this shop of Jane's.

Yesterday, Berto and Grant double-signed a cheque and posted it to the man who owns the second-hand Cessna. A down-payment (of Jane's money) to demonstrate their intentions. They are still setting up a loan with the bank which will take a couple of weeks, but Grant is to collect the aeroplane from Cork on Sunday, and Berto is to meet him at the local airfield.

Familiarity breeds contempt and all that. It is awful how protracted proximity to Jane and Berto irritates me. I find myself chopping off thoughts for fear I will say them. Dylan, from his position of isolation, would use ugly words like compromise and contamination to describe my hesitancies, my disinclination to hurt, my sense of responsibility towards them. Whereas Rohan would advocate hypocrisy provided that there was a good outcome in view. Like money.

I remember that at the beginning of the summer, I thought I had come home temporarily. To recover. I should never have done that. It was like falling off a moving bus. I can't get back on. I'm snared. And now that everybody is believing in everybody else, the atmosphere is as cosy and harmonious as could be. Nothing could go wrong. They are unassailable in this mood. And now they are so buoyant, they are turning on me. "Tell me, Lizzie," Jane said this morning, while we were drinking coffee during a lull. "Is there anything that *does* interest you?"

Berto says I should be thinking about marriage. If I'm not interested in a job, then I should marry. Plenty of fish in the sea, but I won't catch them unless I put out some hooks and a little bait.

They are hurt that I am not content with their solutions.

"We worry about you, Lizzie. You seem to have no idea of what you want to do with yourself."

"I am writing in my spare time," I said defensively, and Jane said, "Oh that," dismissively.

I had a letter from my father in answer to mine, advising me to make up my mind soon about college before I miss the chance of a place this year. I seem to be, he says, in flight from something more serious. It is time I determined to do something.

Why should he presume to know what's best for me now, when he never bothered with me before?

"I might go back to Trinity."

Jane was horrified. "But Lizzie. Four years? At your age? Don't you think a secretarial course might be better?"

She thinks America has ruined me. It has made me over-critical and has given me odd ideas. "You can't live here the way you lived in America. People won't like it. You won't be accepted."

They live in such a tiny, circumscribed world. I don't know how they imagine others exist. Thousands of Janes and Bertos populating the country. Janes and Bertos of all ages.

"I'll leave at the end of the summer. Stay with Tara." And to placate Jane, I added that Tara had a couple of schemes, which was untrue but very comforting to Jane. But she still said, "Are you sure now? You know you'd be more than welcome to stay on. We love having you with us."

"Oh Jane, you'll say the right thing up to the death, won't you?"

"You know you're part of the family. Like a daughter," she insisted.

"Like one but not the same as."

"You are impossible."

"Exactly."

I don't reinforce their way of life, which makes me a

difficult long-term guest.

I have been thinking about Dylan and wishing he was the sort of person who would enable me to put Rohan to the back of my mind. But he's not. I was embarrassed by the way he spoke the other day. It is all very true, I know. I will forget him. But it is not my fault. He has deliberately made himself forgettable. He refuses to give any impression of himself. But perhaps he was even more forgettable before, when he was a sort of acquiescent cog in society. Oh dear. Perhaps people will remember him for his animals. What's-his-name who does the animals. I expect we're all afraid of being forgotten. That's why I clung to Rohan. It's why Jane and Berto stick so closely to one another. Even Dad. He keeps in touch. Small, dry letters, signed as ever, Dad. Whatever else, I am as ever, Dad. But really, our connections with people are so tenuous it is frightening to realise how easily one can slip below memory.

Sunday

I remember thinking this morning, as I looked out through the rippled, blue-tinged glass of the venetian window on the half-landing, that the weather was perfect for flying. Unless one could have too much sun. The cluster of young birch trees by the fence adjoining the two acre paddock stood like golden spears. Upright, poised and shimmering. Berto's line of parched, dead chestnut sticks shrank in their hopeless rows and the sprinkler, which had failed to sustain the trees, lay curled nearby in an indolent, soft, green coil.

And I remember Jane running back from the car to the house to collect a scarf in case she should be called upon to breach the sky in an aeroplane. In the car, driving round the bay, I was lethargically, beautifully overheated. Buried in the soft, fawn leather of the Rover, I slouched, with my eyes half-closed and the sun shining in on my hair. I scarcely listened to Berto and Jane, whose excitement was like boiling, turbulent water. The purchase of an aeroplane opened up such possibilities. Like flight. Jane's hand drifted round the back of Berto's neck, fingers circling on his skin.

Berto was talking in lazy, aggrieved tones. "Look at

those houses," he was saying, while Jane's fingers probed muscles and tendons. "None of them more than three years old. And no taxes. Poverty of the farmers how are you. And that herd of Charollais out there. Fetch thousands." He sighed, and moved his head from side to side, cat-like against Jane's hand. "Big farmers. Little farmers. Own the country."

I hate it when he talks that way. Coming from him, it sounds so cynical.

Their voices descended to murmurs after that, and possibly I fell asleep, for I remember nothing else.

The airfield looked bleak, even in the sun. A couple of aeroplanes which looked as though they might be about to fold their wings, hang their heads and die. They were old-fashioned, rusting in parts, and Jane and I glanced at one another apprehensively, wondering which was the bargain plane. Berto rather thought that one of them was the hired plane in which he had flown with Nick and the photographer, but he couldn't be sure. The other, we decided, was too big.

There was a pre-fabricated concrete shed (on which a number of obscenities were written) at the end of a stretch of tarmacadam towards which we wandered, in the vague hope that behind it might be concealed the Cessna. A present, hidden from view to increase the suspense. But the back of the shed was a dump. A pile of scrap iron, a defunct coffee machine, about fifty crates of empty milk bottles. Jane even peered through the windows into the shed and said that there was nothing inside either.

The heat, which had been pleasant, even enticing at home, was overpowering here. It reflected undauntedly up from the tarmacadam, and pulsed off the walls of the shed. Berto, looking uneasy, patted at his neck with a handkerchief. "Mustn't be here yet." He spoke in a definite voice and looked at his watch.

"Of course, Cork is a long way," Jane ventured. She had hooded her eyes with her hands and was squinting up at the sky.

"Wrong direction, Jane. You're looking north."

"Oh well, no wonder," and she turned direction abruptly. "Oh, the sun's shocking."

I walked around to the front of the shed again. I had the desire to laugh. "Are you sure we have the right Sunday, Berto?" I heard Jane asking as I disappeared round the edge of the shed.

A car was in sight, driving over the stone track towards the tarmacadam. One of those expensive Fords. A man in a cap and a short-sleeved shirt. Elbow out the window, a cigarette in his mouth. He stopped when he drew level with me.

"You looking for someone?" he asked, shouting above the volume of his radio.

"Yes. Mr. Grant."

"Mr. Grant?" He looked puzzled and then he remembered. "Oh. You mean Nick?"

I nodded. "Nick."

"I thought Nick had gone."

"What do you mean, gone?"

"Back to England."

"Oh, but we're supposed to be meeting him here today."

He turned down the radio. "Then he couldn't have gone, could he? My mistake. But I'm pretty sure he said he was leaving last week." He shrugged. "Memory failing me. Funny place to meet someone though."

"He's bringing a plane up from Cork."

I was leaning against the car, enjoying the shudder from its engine. It was one of those loose cars which seemed to shake in all its joints with vibration. The driver shook his head.

"No planes coming in today."

"How do you know?"

"All flights have to be verified by me."

"But perhaps he forgot."

He shook his head again. "Wouldn't be able to leave Cork without notifying me."

"There wouldn't be a message in the shed?"

"There wouldn't."

Jane and Berto were walking over the track towards us. Jane was untying the scarf which she had wrapped around her hair, and Berto was again glancing at his watch as though it might reveal something important. He was looking annoyed.

"Relations?"

"Yes."

"Not too happy."

"No. I think I'd better tell them he's not coming."

"Nor will be. Reckon he's gone back to England."

He looked at me and at Jane and Berto who were coming closer and stumbling on the stones. They looked middle-aged. He was speculating on all sorts of relationships, but then he apparently decided it wasn't his business and revved up the engine.

"Must be moving."

I stood back from the car. "Thanks for your help," I called out, but I don't think he heard me.

Dust rose round the car and Jane and Berto turned their faces away as he passed them by. Jane pulled her scarf up to her eyes.

"Well?" she said, as she reached me.

"Well," I said. "He's gone back to England. Last week."

"But he couldn't have," they both said together.

"He's supposed to be here today."

"What do you mean, Lizzie?" Berto's face was pale, slightly sweaty with the tension of waiting and the heat of the sun.

"I believe, Berto, that he has disappeared with Jane's money."

"Nonsense. He's my partner."

"Was your partner."

It is not that Berto is obtuse. It is simply that as well as being optimistic, he had grown to like Grant. He is always overcome by people's good points, and Nick, he was convinced, had many.

"Is there any point in waiting here, Lizzie?" Jane was dusting her face with the scarf, not thinking of what she was doing at all.

"No."

"We'll go round to his lodgings. See what's happened to him. Perhaps he's sick."

Jane and I looked at one another.

"Why not?" Jane said.

And of course he wasn't at his lodgings in Ennis. He had left during the previous week, with no forwarding address.

Berto had run up the path and had knocked agitatedly on the front door, and the landlady had appeared, wearing a coat, either on her way to or coming home from Mass. Jane and I, watching from the car, could see her shaking her head.

"Poor Berto. Poor, poor Berto,"Jane kept repeating, as we observed them in conversation.

The landlady was sorry Grant had left. He had livened up the house a bit. The jokes. He was a scream, so he was. Kept them in fits and never any trouble about money. Paid on the dot. No. She'd never heard any talk about an aeroplane. Phone-calls to Cork? Come on now, what did he think she was? Some class of a detective? She wasn't one to pry into the doings of her guests. Privacy is the great thing. Lodgers appreciate privacy. Friend he might be, but then again, how was she to know? She had only his word for it. And you'd have thought that Mr. Grant would have let his friends know he was leaving. Really she had nothing more to tell him. And that was that.

"So now what do we do?"

It was an awkward morning. The futility of the same repeated protestations. He couldn't have ... He'll have left a message ... How could he?

"I think we should at least go home for lunch," Jane suggested, and Berto agreed. He thought he might ring a few people after lunch, and make some enquiries.

There we were, all three of us, dressed with gaiety for flight, and there was to be no plane. The money presumably gone. We were silent on the way home. No one spoke. Berto turned on the radio to catch the news headlines, but even that seemed too much for him and he turned it off again. Jane's hand did not caress the back of his neck.

After lunch, Berto disappeared to his study to ring banking friends. Jane and I opened the shop. Walking down the drive, Jane asked me to say nothing, and when I blushed, for there was really nothing to say, she unexpectedly turned on me. She accused me of seeing the pair of them as two-dimensional charades. Laughable. Unreal. She said I had no real sympathy. I simply saw other people through my own code of reference. I never tried to see them as they actually were. She knew what I was thinking of them, she said, and that I was secretly laughing at the way in which they had created yet another mess, but surely even I could see that there was no point to anything unless she and Berto were both happy. And she couldn't be happy if Berto wasn't happy and if I couldn't see that, why, she felt very sorry for me and I had a lot to learn. And when I asked if Berto's happiness was the only prerequisite for her own happiness, she didn't bother to answer. As though I had gone too far.

A group of people were waiting outside the door of the shop, so that we were unable to talk further. But I felt shocked. Rebuffed. It's not as though I've ever said that much.

Berto did not concede that his partner had vanished until four o'clock.

I was at the till by the door when he came into the shop, looking flattened. Really despondent.

"Where's Jane?"

"Over there."

I gestured with my head to where she was standing with a customer by a shelf, gathering up some glasses. She had immersed herself in work for the afternoon, and we hadn't really spoken since we had come inside. Now she looked questioningly at Berto. He made a face and shook his head rapidly.

"Gone. So far as I can tell. I talked to Tim. Cheque cashed at the end of last week. Virtually untraceable, he says."

"Help me to wrap these glasses, will you?"

In silence, they swathed the six crystal glasses.

After the customer had departed, she and Berto murmured to one another, and then came over to me.

"Would you mind holding fort for the rest of the afternoon, Lizzie?"

Jane was obviously disturbed by Berto's appearance. As though it was somehow her fault. Her voice shook.

"Not at all."

"You are an angel."

And they disappeared.

I decided, when I had closed the shop, to go for a swim. I didn't want to intrude further.

The evening was very warm, and the small, white, birdlike clouds which had been dabbling in the blue of the sky throughout the day were now tinged pink and gold and looked altogether more exotic.

At the rocky shelf, beyond the lagoon, a man was dragging plastic bagfuls of seaweed up over the stones, up to a field where he had parked a tractor and trailer. The sea was gentle, undulating against the stones, and I was regretting the summer which didn't happen. The summer of my imagination. My own dream.

The beach shelves very steeply, and the stones under water are slippery and difficult to tread on. It is impossible to enter the water slowly. One is catapulted by the shifting stones. After the first shock of the bitter, evening water, I became acclimatised and even began to feel warm. I lay on my back with my hair plunging down into the water like seaweed hanging from a stone and I drifted, kicking occasionally with my feet to keep on course.

I was considering Berto and Jane, wondering how much there was to think about. Feeling confused to boredom by them. Sometimes it seems that they are just empty shells. Large shells, with complicated, whirling surface patterns but only a few grains of dried sand within. Maybe the occasional, temporary sheltering insect of an idea. I used to think that Jane would eventually be driven over the edge by Berto. I thought she would eventually see through him and be unable to cope. But now I see that she may be much stronger than that. It may be that she has always known exactly what Berto is. But that she has dreamt a dream of how her life should be and she is creating that dream. Her life's work. The creation and maintenance of a dream. Then I was considering myself and wondering was I that much different.

I had forgotten to bring a towel, and having scraped off the water as best I could with my hands, I climbed, with sticky difficulty, back into my clothes, and walked back up the beach to the grass and the following mud-flats. Stranded, silver jellyfish lay melting by the high line of seaweed. Summer seemed in disarray.

It was late when I came upon Berto and Jane walking arm in arm through the garden. The garden, after the heat and the deception of the day, appeared cool, stretched with shadows and delicately screened sunlight. They seemed very close. Almost content. Almost in connivance. Berto still looked wan, and so, to be truthful, did Jane. But the overriding impression was one of peace. Jane was carrying a pair of garden scissors and was cutting the occasional rose. Berto held a small bunch of gathered roses in his hand.

"Beautiful, aren't they?" Jane asked inconsequentially as I joined them. "Do smell them." And Berto dutifully held up the bunch towards my face.

"Of course, the best time to cut flowers," Jane was saying, "is in the early morning, when the dew is still on them. But there you are. They're lovely even now."

Jane has the ability of appearing to immerse herself completely in small happenings. Berto was standing with his arm still linked through hers, drawing small semi-circles on the gravelled path with his foot.

"It all seems so unfair, you know," Berto said, but he sounded resigned rather than angry, and Jane drew her arm more closely round his waist and murmured, "Mmm."

Berto laid his head down on hers, and the roses hung from his hand.

"Sometimes," he said, "I think that there is no reason to anything, but I suppose that there is, somewhere, a plan, which includes you and me, Jane."

It is such a comfortable way in which to view the mess of mistakes which one makes. It absolves one so fully from responsibility.

They began to walk back towards the house, and I followed slowly behind them, passing by the line of wrinkled sticks. Berto poked at one with his foot and sighed, but said nothing. The two of them looked so poignant, leaning on one another. Fragile but indivisible, and I conceded that yes, perhaps there were more layers involved than I could imagine.